This is a work of fiction. Similarities to are entirely coincidental.

SHOOTING STARS IN THE SUM

First edition. August 18, 2023.

Copyright © 2023 Francisco Angulo de Lafuente.

ISBN: 979-8223970682

Written by Francisco Angulo de Lafuente.

The German ace Erwin Maier, decorated three times with the Iron Cross, was shot down and had to parachute from his Messerschmitt BF 109 fighter. When captured by Soviet troops, he asked to be allowed to see the Russian ace who had shot him down. When she came before him, Lydia, a petite young woman with a child's face, thought they were mocking her.

Lydia Litvyak
The White Rose of Stalingrad

Shooting Stars in the Summer Sky

One can only see clearly with the heart; what is essential is invisible to the eyes.

"What is essential is invisible to the eyes," the little prince repeated.

Antoine de Saint-Exupéry

Foreword

Francisco Angulo's ambitious work of historical fiction, Shooting Stars in the Summer Sky, vividly brings to life the daring adventures of intrepid aviators in 1930s Spain, while also portraying a poignant forbidden love story between two young gay men against the dramatic backdrop of the Spanish Civil War.

This sweeping epic masterfully interweaves the exhilarating exploits of fighter pilots racing across the skies with a secret romance that blossoms despite daunting odds. Through rich details and evocative writing, Angulo transports the reader to the volatile period leading up to the devastating war that tore Spain apart.

Critics have praised Angulo's adeptness in capturing the thrilling bravado of the aviators who gripped the nation's imagination while also sensitively delineating the tenderness and passion of the two protagonists defying convention. Hailed as "gripping" and "heart-wrenching," Angulo's novel has drawn comparisons to celebrated wartime classics chronicling the Lost Generation.

Like Hemingway and Dos Passos, Angulo creates an immersive experience through tightly woven prose intermingling adrenaline-fueled aerial action with quiet stolen moments between the young lovers. The result is a beautifully rendered portrait of courage and devotion in the face of adversity.

By turns exhilarating, heartbreaking and insightful, Shooting Stars in the Summer Sky announces an audacious new talent. With captivating characters and evocative historical details, Angulo's masterful storytelling shines a poignant light on human bravery and perseverance in hard times. This stunning novel offers a fresh perspective on sacrifice, honor and the enduring power of love in the midst of conflict.

Warning

SHOOTING STARS IN THE Summer Sky is a historical fiction novel. Many of the events that actually occurred do not match temporally or geographically. The characters' names have been changed. If any of them match real people, it would be purely coincidental.

At the end of this book an explanatory annex has been added on basic aerial combat maneuvers used at that time. The age of propellers, when piston engine aircraft – Hispano-Suiza, Daimler-Benz or Rolls-Royce Merlin – dominated the skies.

Prologue

Richard Beckenbauer suffers an unfortunate accident at the Berlin Grand Prix, his flaming car crashes into the grandstand where top military commanders and Adolf Hitler himself are located. He is accused of being a terrorist and sent to prison awaiting trial. Badly injured, with broken legs, and with only minimal medical attention from a nurse, he begins to see life in a different way, every night he dreams of flying over golden fields of wheat and rye. When his brother dies, he is offered a mission in Almeria, Spain, if he reports on the plans of revolutionary, union, anarchist and communist leaders, his file will be cleared, and he is also promised he can return to racing.

Tomás García Hernández, anarchist leader, writer, poet and above all aviator, will be his mentor, the instructor who will teach him to fly, to see life through different eyes. The universal love that knows no borders. The forbidden and clandestine love between two young people. The inner war first and then the other, the war in Spain. The fratricidal struggle between brothers, demolishing families, turning the uprooted person into a relentless killer.

The exploitation, misery and hunger, inhuman working conditions in the mines that led workers to their deaths. The revolutionary strikes by peasants, day laborers and miners. The exodus of the population and the massacre on the Málaga highway and later the bombing ordered by Adolf Hitler on the city of Almeria.

Dying for the dream of a better world, glimpsed obliquely in poems by Lorca, Machado and Hernández, with a broken voice and the sound of a guitar. The ideals of young pilots who give their lives for freedom, shooting stars in the summer sky.

Chapter 1

Dreaming of Flying

LYING IN A BED IN THE prison infirmary, with broken legs and internal injuries that were draining his life away, he began to dream of flying. The feeling of being as free as the wind, but sooner or later you always have to wake up and return to the harsh reality. If you have money, you can pay for good doctors and lawyers, but Richard had invested everything in the races, in preparing his car. He had always loved challenges, he was able to face death with calm and serenity, entering every curve without braking and stepping on the accelerator at the exit. Since the dawn of humanity it has been like this, the strong have always taken advantage of the weak, imposing their rules. Richard Beckenbauer was not one of them: Arrogant and fanatical Nazi followers of Adolf Hitler.

From his bed he looked at the flaking grayish white paint on the ceiling. Minutes seemed like hours, hours like days, and the endless days followed one after the other. His very light greenish blue eyes had lost their shine. In the prison infirmary, there were only two beds, and the other was occupied by common prisoners with various minor illnesses: dysentery, colic, diarrhea and scabies. Richard had both legs in casts, several broken ribs, bandaged burnt hands, a swollen and bruised face. His condition was dire. After the accident, no one would give a Reichsmark "Imperial Mark" for him. Against all odds he was determined to live. His heart, still in his twenties - he wasn't even thirty yet - strong and stubborn, kept him going.

On Sundays a young nurse was in charge of the dispensary. Richard could hear Marlene Dietrich's voice coming out of the Volksempfänger, a small rectangular wooden radio designed by Otto Griessing for Seibt. Her songs were the only thing that broke the sterile monotony of the infirmary.

Whenever he tried to move even just to change position, he felt stabbing pains all over his body. He had bedsores on his back, ulcers from lying still for so long.

On January 30, 1933, President Paul von Hindenburg appointed Adolf Hitler Chancellor, granting him full powers. This eliminated any legal objections that could be made by opposition parties. With the loss of the First World War, the German people had been suffocated by the reparation and compensation policies of the victorious nations. The only way to cope was to go further and further into debt, with foreign loans. American money produced a bubble, a fictitious recovery of the economy that would burst, plunging Germany into absolute misery. This was the breeding ground for the rage and xenophobia that brought the Nazis to power.

After months of recovery he finally felt strong enough to go outside for some fresh air. With crutches and a leg in a cast. The courtyard of Plötzensee prison was surrounded by red brick walls that only allowed you to look up at the sky; a leaden sky in black and white. Richard Beckenbauer leaned against one of the walls and after months in bed once again felt the cold damp air of Berlin. For the moment that was enough for him, he didn't think beyond that, nor did he care about the future, or what would happen tomorrow.

"Do you have a cigarette?" he asked a young man, almost a boy, who was standing nearby smoking nervously with a frightened look on his face.

He took out a crumpled pack of Sorte cigarettes, red with a big number one in the center. He offered one and handed over the cigarette he had between his lips so Richard could use it to light the other one. The boy was also awaiting trial for distributing pamphlets on the campus of Humboldt University, criticizing the repressive policies of the Nazis.

"Don't smoke too much. German doctors have recently confirmed it is a direct cause of cancer deaths." Richard winked at him with a faint smile, as if anyone cared about damn cancer under those circumstances. He turned towards the entrance of the pavilion before the siren sounded ending outdoor time.

He had not walked more than two meters when a fat man with a surly look and the appearance of a repeat offender approached the university student in a threatening manner.

"Give me the cigarette pack or I'll knock your teeth out, princess, so you can suck better on the cripple."

When he refused, the man grabbed him by the neck with one hand and slapped him hard with the other open hand. Richard Beckenbauer limped over on crutches with his leg in a cast held high, grabbed the bottom of the wooden crutch and smashed it on the man's head. When he turned to hit Richard, Beckenbauer, lame in one leg and the other paralyzed, furiously pounced on him, knocking him to the ground and relentlessly punching him in the face. He left the man's face covered in blood, his thick nicotine-stained mustache turned red. Two prison guards grabbed Richard by the arms and tossed him into a muddy puddle as if he were a rag doll. They ordered the prisoners inside and closed the courtyard doors, leaving Richard lying in the rain and mud. His light brown hair, almost blond, darkened as it became soaked with water. The intense cold chilled him to the bone, making him shiver, but he made no attempt to get up, nothing mattered to him anymore.

Chapter 2

The Grand Prix

DRIVING ONE OF THE silver arrows "Silberpfeile" was every racer's dream. Nazi Germany was determined to show the world what they were capable of, an unequivocal sign of Aryan superiority. The automotive industry, Auto Union and Mercedes Benz, were ordered to manufacture the best racing cars in the world. The best machines and drivers came together at the Nürburgring circuit. Built in the 1920s as a testing site for German car brands, it was designed by Otto Creutz and in 1927 hosted the German Grand Prix. The original layout was twenty-eight point three kilometers long and was considered the most complicated and difficult circuit in the world. Formula 1 driver Jackie Stewart nicknamed it the "Green Hell." After 1929, the full layout was no longer used. The winning drivers of the 1930s were called Ringmeister, "Masters of the Circuit." Among them: Rudolf Caracciola, Tazio Nuvolari and Bernd Rosemeyer.

The car flew off the ground on all four wheels at every change of gradient. Richard Beckenbauer drifted into the tight banked curves. The cigar-shaped cars had barely any aerodynamic lift, they lacked fins and wings. Richard was in third place, trying to overtake one of the silver arrows, an Auto Union. A Mercedes Benz was leading, he was the only non-factory team driver running among the leaders. He had invested all his effort, work and savings into preparing that car. Painted black with the words "Bullet Schwarz" in gold, The Black Bullet was very fast, as he had modified the engine himself. In the fifth lap the expected battle was already underway, on the finish line the team directors recorded times stopwatch in hand. The circuit surface varied depending on the section, tight narrow concrete curves near the stands, more open and bumpy through the green wooded mountainous area. There were spectators of all kinds and social classes, elegant men and women in the boxes and stands near the finish line, wearing jackets, flannel pants, white shirts and bow ties or neckties for men and exquisite tight-fitting Parisian fashion dresses for women. Then sitting on the grass of the hillsides, entire families with blankets on the ground, food and drink as if on a picnic. Rich and poor, men, women and children, got to their feet when they heard the roar of the engines approaching. Before reaching the carousel, Richard attempted a new overtaking maneuver. His car was inferior in top speed, so he had to take chances entering the curves faster and braking much later, hence his characteristic driving style, drifting from side to side, crossing the car over the central axis of the track. He wasn't a well-known driver, this was the first time he was fighting for a podium finish in a Grand Prix. Up until now his only goal had been to finish the races. Nevertheless some fans had already noticed him, calling him "Brennende Räder" Burning Wheels, because of his peculiar way of driving. Lap after lap, the three leaders were pulling away from the rest of the field by five seconds. For his single seater the competition was becoming increasingly difficult, the wheels were screeching on every curve, the engine had begun to lose more oil than usual and the brakes were overheating. The engine coolant temperature gauge had been in the red for several laps.

The Mercedes silver arrow set a new circuit record lap speed. Beckenbauer knew he couldn't let this opportunity pass, even if he blew up his engine he was capturing everyone's attention, team directors included. That could mean a huge leap forward, the coveted contract with one of the big brands. He gritted his teeth on the entry to each curve, pushing the little tire rubber left to the limit. If he pitted now to change tires he would lose many positions that would be very difficult to recover. He decided to push on no matter what, hoping his car would last the final five laps. The silver cars were running nose to tail on the straights, almost touching wheels. Rudolf closed the door on the Mercedes Benz at the carousel entry, the two vehicles made contact. The Auto Union's front right wheel pushed the rear of the Mercedes, causing it to lose control. The single seater spun wildly as the crowd shrieked in terror. Richard met it head on and narrowly avoided a collision by zigzagging his car. This maneuver moved him up into second place. Now he had to squeeze every ounce of power from his engine.

Rudolf recovered from the incident losing just a few seconds. Beckenbauer watched helplessly as the silver single seater closed in on him, meter by meter. He kept it behind him, closing the door on every overtaking attempt. His car may not have been the best - that was obvious - but he was willing to leave his skin and soul on this circuit. The two of them were catching up to the Mercedes in the lead. With two laps to go, the three drivers were battling for victory. In the grandstand even Adolf Hitler himself was standing expectantly watching the thrilling race. Richard wiped away the small dark droplets of engine oil spattering on his goggles. His face was blackened from the smoke coming out of his engine. At that moment he recalled how hard it had been to get there: the grueling workshop days, the endless testing before each race, this was a full time commitment, there was nothing else in his life. A leather helmet, pilot goggles and an oil-stained overall were his sole belongings, he didn't even own the car, he owed it to investors and lenders. The walls of the rented room in his Berlin apartment, were covered in photos tacked up with thumbtacks. Racing cars and great champions on the podium with a laurel wreath over their shoulders. He had been working in the mechanic workshop since he was twelve, preparing several cars for amateur competitions. Old production cars that he modified himself, souping up the engines, lightening the bodywork and reinforcing the chassis. Many of his friends had lost their lives in accidents. Most roads were gravel and dirt tracks, full of potholes and holes. People didn't understand his passion for speed, calling them crazy. Reckless kids risking their lives with beat up old cars.

With less than two laps to go, he continued to fiercely defend second place. The tires without rubber were causing the rear of the single seater to skid. Rudolf's Auto Union had ample power to overtake, but unless it sprouted wings, Richard Beckenbauer wasn't going to let him by. The three of them approached the finish line to start the final lap. There was an explosion, followed by fire and black smoke, the car was in flames and he couldn't see anything. Then he lost control. That was the last thing he remembered before waking up in the hospital bed. His vehicle rolled over several times and flew off towards the grandstand, the presidential box where Adolf Hitler was located along with several army commanders and prominent German businessmen. A wheel struck the officer on Hitler's right side, seriously injuring him. Fortunately he didn't die, because in that case Richard's fate would have taken very different turns. The race was suspended and an exhaustive investigation carried out to determine the cause of the accident, in case it was one, since the Nazis had accused Beckenbauer of being a terrorist. It was an absurd accusation, no one can plan an attack posing as a racing driver, only to then kill himself by crashing his car into the stands. Of course that would have to be determined by a court and there would be no trial if the Nazis didn't authorize it. It was enough to find out that Richard Beckenbauer's mother was Spanish, to have him transferred from the hospital to the Plötzensee prison infirmary. Deprived of freedom and stripped of his professional racing license - the latter hurt him even more - awaiting the verdict of a Nazi court that would pass sentence.

Chapter 3

The Island of Rügen

HE REMAINED LYING IN the courtyard mud puddle, half frozen, absent, not feeling or suffering, looking at the infinite gray sky and the fine raindrops falling on his face. He heard the metallic door bolt of the pavilion building slide open and the sound produced by the hard leather soles of the two men's shoes as they approached him. Both were wearing black suits with pinstripes, navy blue ties, long dark brown overcoats and felt hats.

"Are you Richard Beckenbauer?" - the captain asked, as if he didn't know. As he extended his hand in a friendly greeting that at the same time helped him get up.

"We have bad news for you." - said the other one. And he continued. - "Your brother has passed away."

They had found him in a Berlin alley, lying in the street near the back door of a brewery, bleeding from several stab wounds. His wallet had been stolen and everything suggested it was a robbery that ended in dramatic consequences. The police were doing everything possible to find the culprit.

"Crime has reached historic highs. Those damned Jewish dogs, who take our money, our women, and are capable of stabbing a man for a handful of bills." - The anti-Semitic comment was made by the younger one.

That kind of comment was common among low-educated Germans. It could be heard in any Berlin dive, amidst a cloud of tobacco smoke and tables full of beer mugs.

His brother had been working on a secret project in Spain, as an engineer at a mine, but also infiltrated among the population, gathering information for Germany. Since he had decided to work for the Nazis, they had barely been in contact. Richard always tried to stay out of political drifts. These were difficult times for independent thinkers. Anyone who disagreed with the Nazis was singled out and ostracized from society. The jails were filling up with innocent people and he was a prime example. The two men in suits seemed full of kind words and noble motives. They proposed that he continue his brother's work, although he knew nothing about mining. It didn't take a genius to figure out what they wanted. The resemblance to his brother was reasonable, but more importantly was his fluent Spanish. His mother was from a town near the mine.

"A clean record, a new life, a fresh start somewhere else, and doing great things for Germany." - The older military man spoke sincerely to him.

"Besides, the pay is good." - The young soldier added.

"Really good, monthly salary, expenses paid, and a bonus at the end of the mission that will allow you to start your own business. I've seen you race. With that money you could return to the circuits." - Both soldiers smiled in a friendly way.

"I don't know if I'll ever walk properly again, and I don't even have a license."

"It's all been thought out, don't worry."

His brother Rudolf Beckenbauer was the engineer, he was the one who wanted to travel to Almeria and do great things for Germany. Richard knew nothing about mines or his brother's troubles in Spain. He didn't have much to think about: stay in jail awaiting trial and then hopefully be transferred to a labor camp; by the time he was free again, if he didn't die of tuberculosis or pneumonia, he would be an old man. The other option was to sign with these Germans, get out of jail, and see what would happen after that.

They transferred him to the island of Rügen, to the Prora vacation complex designed for rewarded Nazi tourists. It was conceived to accommodate twenty thousand tourists. All the rooms had views of the Baltic Sea beach. The eight buildings lined up at the edge of the beach stretched over four kilometers, forming a gigantic concrete structure. He was provided 24-hour medical care, daily appointments with the doctor, two nurses assigned to him, and a doctor who acted as his personal trainer, forcing him every morning to do rehabilitation exercises. After six months he was in better shape than ever. When walking he had a slight limp that doctors assured would disappear over time. He weighed a bit more as he had gained muscle mass. His hair was lighter from the seawater and sun, and the eyes had regained their particular glow. His facial skin had some color, giving him a healthy look. He was tall and athletic, attractive to the point of capturing the attention of single and married women who ogled him over their husbands, even on their honeymoon. Prora was a nice place to spend a vacation, but after the first few months the crowds of families with crying children became tiresome. Gambling, alcohol and tobacco were prohibited, his only entertainment was walking. Conversations with doctors and nurses were banal, people were careful not to get into politics or talk about the economy. The Nazi symbolism was an eyesore, long strips of red fabric hung like flags with huge printed crosses could be seen everywhere. Stone coats of arms on the facades like medieval shields with an eagle carrying a laurel wreath and inside the swastika.

Chapter 4

The Mines of Rodalquilar

SINCE HE WAS A CHILD, his mother told him about her land, but when she died when he was ten and went to live with his grandparents in Berlin, he thought he would never travel to Spain.

The Rodalquilar mining complex was located on top of an ancient volcano, on the caldera that collapsed due to the magma chamber failure. The collapse caused the material to spread throughout the basin. From the window of the Junkers Ju 52 he saw for the first time that unique landscape more akin to Mars or Venus, mountains and rivers of red, blue, purple, yellow and black mud. Large tunnels had been dug to cut the veins and be able to work the extracted rock better. There were seven active mines at the same time:

The Consulta mine had been in operation since the early twentieth century. Vein 340 was one of the excavations in the same rock and although it was initially discarded due to its low mineral content, it later proved to be one of the most productive where a new mineral called rodalquilarite was also found, located near the Denver plant, two kilometers to the west. The María Josefa mine was the first mine where the precious mineral was found that did not require prior treatment to be extracted, simple sieving and separation were all that was needed. In 1925 Juan López Soler had facilities built at the entrance to process the extracted rock on site. But when heating the material for separation, mixtures of chemicals were obtained that made it unfeasible, leading him to fail a year later. The Las Niñas mine, one of the largest sets of galleries and facilities, was located one kilometer south of the central base and was already active producing lead in the 19th century. The mineral was taken to the beach and from there by boat to Mazarrón, to be processed at the Santa Elisa foundry and obtain gold lead ingots. The Abellán mine, in 1929 Antonio Abellán invested his entire fortune in the construction of a new plant to carry out the complete gold ore processing on the Las Yeguas ravine. Once again it failed due to the low skills of the miners and the poor state of the art. The La Ronda mine where the galleries descended to more than forty meters deep. Dorr Plant, it began operating around 1930 and had the first cyanidation processing plant in the area. It processed a large amount of material until 1936.

The stripped land, with its entrails exposed, looked like a World War I battlefield that he had seen in photos. Craters of different sizes from artillery shells dotted the entire area. The advanced German technology was demonstrating its potential. Modern pneumatic tools, excavators and trucks. They built a runway next to the mine, where the Junkers had landed bumping up and down.

The newcomers were gathered in the conference room, where the manager, a small man with a sweat-soaked white shirt and crooked, loosened tie, gave them a talk explaining the rules and warning them of the dangers.

"Don't trust those young Republican, anarchist and communist women out there, they're waiting for you to lower your guard so they can stab you in the back."

He was a businessman. Behind his metal-rimmed glasses, small, black, evil eyes were hidden. An ant that worked on its own, accumulating everything.

"And wrap it up, those whores will give you diseases that will kill you without you even realizing it."

In Germany those men had wives and children, reputation, they were exemplary citizens. Here they frequented bars and brothels.

Once the welcoming talk was over, he headed down the central corridor to where the bedrooms were located. It was a large complex, with several barracks for the workers and individual small houses for managers and officers. A tall, extremely thin young man approached him.

"Beckenbauer?" - He scrutinized him pensively.

"Richard" - He shook his hand greeting him.

"You look a lot like your brother. By the way, I'm very sorry, please accept my sincere condolences."

Michael Horten was one of the engineers, coworker and friend of his brother. He gave Richard a tour showing him the facilities. He also explained the operation of the mine in general terms. He showed Richard to his room and a small desk with a Mercedes brand typewriter on it, which he found quite ironic. He received orders to type a daily report detailing the contacts he had, when, how and with whom he had spoken. That was his only task, to mill around the vicinity and submit meaningless reports.

Horten took him to the meeting room, where a woman was nervously smoking and reviewing documents on the table. She was blonde, with chin-length wavy hair styled to one side, very fashionable for the thirties. She was probably seven or eight years older than him. This was Professor Diane Klum, a psychiatrist and social behavior doctor, although here she taught young children and ran the local school, or at least that was her cover. As soon as they walked into the room, Michael started speaking Spanish to her, but his command and pronunciation were terrible.

"What are you doing here?" - She was upset, in a bad mood. - "You don't have the slightest idea about the work your brother was doing."

"I'm sorry it was my brother who died." - If it was a divine decision, it didn't seem to be a very wise one. His brother was a hardworking and educated man, willing to improve the lives of others; on the other hand, all he knew was driving fast.

"We've been working on this project for years and they send us a crazy race car driver..." I'm going to talk to the top brass to get this guy out of here. " - She took an angry drag on her cigarette and threw it on the floor before leaving the room.

She didn't waste a second, rushed out of the building and headed uphill to where the loaded trucks were coming down from the mine. That's where the manager was, the little man in oversized clothes who always had a bitter expression on his face.

"I'm not taking over that racer." - Now she was really pissed off.

She wouldn't stop protesting having to incorporate Richard into her group. But the manager paid no attention to her, he was focused on hitting the little golf ball with his eight iron. Diane held her breath for a few seconds as if she was about to explode at any moment. The manager's biology did not seem compatible with the Almeria climate, his white skin had an intense red color, from sun and heat. He had thrown the tie over his left shoulder in preparation for the swing. His "Address" stance was correct before launching the ball towards the multicolored mounds of earth piled on the hillside. The doctor kept on shouting and barking like a dog, while the little man remained impassive. With sober parsimony he stuck the tee into the ground and placed the ball on top. Before he could make a new swing, Diane Klum kicked the ball, sending it rolling down the hillside.

"Well, I think we've been very lucky, the resemblance to his brother plus he speaks perfect Spanish. Where do you think we'll find another one like that?" - He handed the iron to the improvised Caddie, the soldier in charge of his personal security, and took a few steps to the right, where they had a table with the mine plans. - "We have to maintain control of the mines at all costs, that ore is essential for Germany. We win the locals over with jobs, food and vaccines for the children, and we even build them a school. And yet the situation continues to deteriorate."

"Of course, that's how it usually goes. You think they're idiots, you exploit their resources, expropriate their wealth, and in return you give them powdered milk for the kids and some measly coins for their parents."

He grabbed the professor by the arm and dragged her over to see the ore they were extracting.

"Do you see this? This is why we're in Spain. This precious metal moves the world. Hitler will make us great again. A powerful and united Germany." - He spoke with increasing fervor, the pinkish tone of his face turned darker red. - "We're on the brink of a damn war, we have to get along with these illiterates. We have to maintain control of the mines at all costs."

Chapter 5

Tungsten

THE MINING EXPLOITATION began in the 16th century at the height of the Reconquest. Large tunnels or open-air trenches were dug from which alum was extracted and used in fixing dyes for fabrics. This mineral was very important during the Middle Ages. Around the year 1520, the first mining village was established. In one of the frequent attacks by Barbary pirates, they kidnapped the entire population of Los Alumbres. To protect the mine and its workers, the Castle of Los Alumbres had to be built near the Playazo road. Since ancient times, mining companies had failed over and over due to lack of technology, but the Nazis had the means. The exploitation of argentiferous lead, prominent in the Santa Barbara mine, reached its peak between 1870 and 1875.

They got ready to go down for a visit to the Rodalquilar school. This was the first contact Richard had with the local population. But Diane was still very reluctant. She was a mature woman who seemed to have very clear ideas, she knew what she wanted, how to proceed at all times, how to act, which path she wanted things to follow.

"What made you come to Spain? You have no idea what the situation is like." - The teacher shook her head slightly, she couldn't understand it.

"I had nothing better to do, and prison life was very monotonous." - He smiled sarcastically.

The second phase of mining exploitation was started by José Manzano Castro in 1897. The Las Niñas mine was about two kilometers from Rodalquilar and was one of the most important in the 19th century, followed by the Demasía and Potosí mines. The precious metal was scattered in the rock and the technology required for extraction was not available at that time. Near the mine, facilities for workers were built, housing, a company store and even a small chapel. The village of San Diego, was accompanied by two other smaller ones. The construction was carried out in 1930 and was equipped with everything necessary for workers and engineers, and even had a laboratory to perform the required tests. The mining base was located on the slopes of Cerro del Cinto, near the crossroads in the Hornillo valley. Just below was the Cortijo del Fraile and then the town of Rodalquilar.

Tungsten, also known as wolfram, was extracted from the mines. It was initially used for manufacturing bulbs with tungsten filaments and also cutting tools, but they soon realized its special properties for weapons production. Armored piercing anti-tank shells and manufacturing new battle tanks. Tungsten was an indispensable element for Nazi Germany and Francoist Spain assured Hitler of the supply. The national ore was present in both world wars. It is a chapter in our history that almost no one talks about, it was kept highly secret for a long time and was key in the Nazis' arms race.

Chapter 6

Commander Uli Lindemann

THAT MORNING AFTER breakfast, he went out to explore the surroundings. Anything with a motor interested him, so after seeing the excavators and trucks at work, he talked to the drivers for a while about engines, displacement, power and other technical details. Then he went to the mine's airfield, where the Junkers Ju 52 was parked while the pilot performed an inspection.

"Good morning. Don't you have mechanics in charge of that job?" - He asked curiously.

"I like to check everything myself. After all, I'm the one risking my life."

Christoph Schneider, the pilot working for the mining company, came from Lufthansa. He was an experienced aviator with many flight hours. Thirty-eight years old, black hair speckled with gray, military style haircut and blue eyes.

"What engines! How many horsepower do they have?" - The three radial engines of the Junkers caught his attention.

"It has three 550 hp Pratt & Whitney Hornet engines, although I've seen the new Luftwaffe ones and they have BMW 132-A-3 engines of 725 hp each."

"Impressive, they should make a car with one of these engines." - He pointed to the left wing engine. Christoph approached, wiping his hands on a rag he took out of his overalls rear pocket, and then shook

Richard's hand. "What I still don't understand is the corrugated sheet metal."

"The corrugated skin was Junkers engineers' idea, providing great strength to the aircraft without adding weight. The only problem is it reduces aerodynamics and sometimes the air passing through the corrugations makes it whistle like a church organ. But it's the safest aircraft I've ever flown, it can stay in the air even after two engines fail. The sturdy fixed landing gear slows it down quite a bit during flight, but you don't have to worry about it getting stuck."

Despite the ironclad restrictions on military equipment imposed on Germany by the Treaty of Versailles, secret projects and military training programs for selected personnel had been carried out since 1919 at secluded facilities outside German territory, mainly in the USSR following the 1922 Treaty of Rapallo. Starting in 1932 when Germany left the peace commissions, a highly confidential rearmament program was initiated. The Luftwaffe would use civilian aircraft that had been designed for that purpose, easily modifiable to transform them into warplanes. The Junkers Ju 52 was one of them, used as a military transport and also as a bomber.

"Do you only fly this aircraft?" - He was referring to flying just for pleasure.

"I have my own small plane at the back of the hangar." - Although in different ways, they were essentially talking about the same thing. Their passion for machines, for speed, the wind on their faces. "I can't stay on the ground for more than a few hours."

A military man came running up the road leading to the airfield. It was Commander Uli Lindemann on his morning workout. Every morning he would run about six miles on the dusty roads near the mine, whether it rained or the sun blazed. He was a tough man, hardened by the battles of World War I. He had a war scar crossing his face, from the left temple down to the corner of his mouth. His hair was completely white with age and he had a thick mustache of the same color. He stopped at the hangar entrance and walked to the back right side, where there was a military green towel hanging from a rivet tail.

"You have to stay in shape, Beckenbauer. If you stay still your muscles will atrophy and when you need to run it will be too late." - He wore a white sleeveless undershirt on top and military pants and boots below, soldier boots, with shoelaces like hiking boots. Officer boots were tall riding boots. "I've seen some of your races, you've got guts, son."

"It's just a job like any other." - He downplayed it.

"Don't believe it. After World War I, after seeing soldiers running through no man's land to attack enemy trenches, I've only seen that expression again, that look, in pilots' eyes. Many of your colleagues have lost their lives on the circuits, you almost did yourself. I need brave, determined people, this mission is damn tough." - He wiped off the sweat with the towel and turned serious. "Look Beckenbauer, the professor and the other bookworms have no idea what we're doing here. I need you to infiltrate those communist dogs. I need a man to inform me of their plans, what's brewing inside. We have to maintain control of the mines, win their friendship, and if they want war, hit them where it hurts most."

Richard felt the commander was speaking to him like a father, paternally. He usually distrusted the military, but this man was different, he spoke bluntly, clearly and directly. He wasn't a crazy fanatic or ambitious politician, he was a battle-hardened soldier, charismatic, who fought for his men and his homeland.

"Can you do that for me? Report everything you see and hear..."

"Of course, commander."

The military man shook his hand in a friendly greeting.

"Uli. Call me Uli." - Richard nodded in agreement and Uli bid him farewell with an approving gesture.

Before leaving he paused briefly.

"Son, I have contacts at Mercedes. What would you think about racing in one of their silver arrows?"

"That would be fantastic" - His eyes lit up.

"You keep me informed of what you find out and consider it done. When you return to Germany you will be part of the best racing team."

Chapter 7

The School

HE TOLD DR. DIANE THAT he would go down to the village with them, that he wanted to meet the people, talk to them to see what they thought. Try to find a solution by mediating between the miners and management. Diane Klum still thought he was an irresponsible madman who would cause them more harm than good. Despite orders from her superiors, she was adamantly opposed to Beckenbauer being part of her team.

"What you have to do is keep your mouth shut. Enjoy your time here as if it were a vacation." - That's how she put it.

When Michael Horten got into the Opel Olympia, Beckenbauer was already behind the wheel. The car looked brand new, cream gray with light brown soft top. Professor Diane Klum rode in the back of the dark green Citroën C4 open bed truck. The winding road downhill caused the Olympia to accelerate. When he reached the first curve it was as if something ignited inside him. He felt long forgotten sensations, buried for almost a year, in his thoughts the certainty that he would never get his hands on a steering wheel again.

"Take it easy, slower! Nooo! Holy Virgin!" - Horten held on as best he could, grabbing the seat base with one hand and the door handle with the other.

He took the curves in his distinctive way, with the style that characterized him in races, drifting the rear of the car and entering sideways. While the skinny engineer riding shotgun tried not to throw up and felt a weakness that made him faint, Richard Beckenbauer came alive again. He couldn't explain it, when accelerating he shifted to another state, another dimension, with its own physical laws, where time is not solid and linear, a second can be a minute and a whole lifetime in one minute. Elastic time, the factual corroboration of Albert Einstein's theory of relativity. Dr. Klum's voice was heard.

"Stop him, stop that madman." - She ordered over the radio.

The orders must have been for Michael, but the man had enough trouble not vomiting or wetting himself. A bump made the compact Opel Olympia jump one meter into the air, the shock absorbers withstood the punishment.

"Oh God, dear God!" - The passenger shouted as they flew.

Beckenbauer never stopped being a driver, he may not have had a car, but he still had gasoline in his veins.

They arrived at the school they had built, to speak with the teachers and see how things were going. The teacher seemed truly interested in the well-being of the people, especially the children, making sure the miners' kids attended school so they would be educated someday. They taught them natural sciences, math, reading and writing in Spanish and German too. Diane taught classes every day, she liked being in contact with the kids to see their progress firsthand. The small single-story building, with whitewashed adobe brick walls and two-sided uralite roof, conveyed a cold feeling, but its interior wallpapered with the children's colorful drawings shone with life.

Richard wasn't terribly interested in the school issue. He broke away from the group and walked around the village of Rodalquilar - it was interesting scenery, but there wasn't much else to see - so he got on a truck heading to the city of Almeria. He spent the afternoon walking the streets, visited the port and ate at an octopus restaurant. Despite the employment situation and large number of unemployed, he was surprised by the bustle in bars, inns and taverns. It was a unique country, full of contradictions and subtle nuances. There may have been a lack of bread, but wine was plentiful. The middle class was virtually non-existent, some went barefoot while others drove a Rolls-Royce or a beautiful Hispano-Suiza. The situation in Spain was dramatic. In Andalusia the land was in the hands of a few large landowners and peasants subsisted in miserable conditions, hired as day laborers in markets, in town squares as if they were cattle. Families living in shacks and caves dug into the ground, malnourished children and exploited men without future prospects. The leftist parties had promised them agrarian reform, dividing up the land among the workers. But the government soon realized it was an impossible task. Experts were sent to all parts of the country to orchestrate said reform. One expert's report was adamant: "There can be no reform without war. No one who owns land is going to just give it away to farmers."

Once the colonies were lost, the military became obsessed with Spain's unity, which was threatened by autonomy demands from Catalans and Basque separatists. With a disproportionate army - there was one officer for every nine soldiers - accustomed to influencing the government, pressure was mounting. On August 10, 1932, Lieutenant General José Sanjurjo's attempted coup fails, heightening discontent among the military. There were several workers' strikes, CNT anarchists in Andalusia promoted revolutionary strikes. Leaders like Tomás García Hernández marched at the forefront, cutting fences on estates to allow laborers to seize them. Because the situation called for it, there were men, women and children starving to death. Fed up with hearing promises from the Republic and seeing no change in the situation, anarchist groups decided to act on their own, rejecting any form of government. In 1933 the revolutionary protests in Casas Viejas ended when police set fire to a house where a group of anarchists had taken refuge. Comrades of Tomás, fellow party members, were burned alive by the fire. Among them was a brother of Pepe Baena, a union leader in Almeria. The Republic was accused of having ordered the police to act. It was clear that the agrarian reform had failed.

In Asturias, miners on strike organized themselves, enjoyed the support of most of the population, and had access to explosives from the mines to face the police. The Republic sent General Francisco Franco, at the head of the Legion and the African army. The uprising was crushed and many of its leaders executed, shot in the streets without any defense or trial. Thousands of miners were jailed.

In 1936, Dolores Ibárruri, a deputy for Asturias, upon taking office immediately called for the release of the miners. But processing the decree could take months, so she went to the jail herself and asked to be handed the keys to the cells. She ran down the corridors opening doors amidst shouts of joy from comrades.

He was truly surprised. Despite the serious situation in the country, people seemed somehow oblivious and happy. There wasn't a tavern without spontaneous singers breaking into bulerías after a swig of wine.

Chapter 8

The Young Anarchist

WHEN HE LEFT THE EL Cortijo tavern, it was already dark, it had gotten late and he had to get back to the mining base. The best thing would be to walk to the town square and get a taxi there. The sky was black, the moon hadn't come out yet, and many of the cobbled alleyways lacked lighting. He stopped for an instant in front of an illuminated window, the yellow kerosene lamp flame in the center of the living room table, around which a family was having dinner. He then realized that the footsteps he heard in the background had also stopped. When he started walking he heard them again, he sped up almost running, confirming he was being followed. He turned into a narrow street on the right and came face to face with a man dressed in black pants and a blue shirt, blocking his path. He couldn't see his face, from his build he was young and he was holding something metallic that glinted in his hand. When Richard turned to go back the way he had come, two other men were waiting for him. All dressed alike, young Falangists who went out at night looking for trouble. He raised his hands as if surrendering, while walking towards the one with the knife. When he got close, before the man could say anything, Richard pushed him and started running. The three chased him down the street. He tried to get to the square as soon as possible, but had to stay hidden, running from corner to corner, from doorway to doorway, crouching in the shadows.

Diane asked an elderly man from Rodalquilar who was sitting at his front door and he told her he had seen a well-dressed young man get on the truck heading to Almeria. She ordered returning to the mining truck and got into the Olympia with Horten. As soon as they arrived in the city, they encountered people whistling at them and yelling insults, apparently the mining executives were not very popular with the locals. A group of kids started throwing stones at them.

"I'm sorry professor, we have to go back." - The engineer told her. "We have orders to be back before nightfall. Richard is a grown man, he knows what he's doing."

"That crazy young pilot has walked into a hornet's nest, caught between two sides. He'll show up tomorrow stabbed or shot dead." - Her words conveyed resignation. They couldn't disobey orders from the top brass.

The young anarchist Tomás García Hernández has him in his sights, aiming at his head with his shotgun. Night clashes between anarchists and Falangists were common throughout the country. Killing a Nazi German who had come to exploit workers, gut the land and leave it all polluted in order to take away its riches didn't seem like a bad idea to him. The effects of contamination on the population and especially on the miners were devastating, many children never got to meet their parents. Respiratory diseases such as pneumoconiosis and silicosis killed workers slowly and silently. With proper equipment, simple masks, it could be avoided, but the mining directors didn't care. Tomás had his index finger on the trigger, he just needed to squeeze it a bit and the German would be done for. He hesitated, he had never killed anyone before, much less an unarmed man, although the party had decided to carry out armed actions. Politics and pleasant words had proven useless. At that moment, both sides thought the same, the only way to make changes required violent acts. He took a deep breath and aimed precisely, although his hand trembled. At the moment he was going to shoot, a small medal of the virgin, a gift from his mother, came out of the neckline of his shirt. He was an anarchist, superstitious and a believer, he took it as some kind of sign, the virgin on the barrel of his shotgun, right before his eyes, on the sights. The three Falangists had discovered him, he no longer needed to make any decision, they would probably slit his throat like a pig. The one with the knife approached him first, with a quick stab to the chest, trying to plunge it in, but with a rapid movement Beckenbauer dodged the blow blocking it with his left forearm while connecting a descending right hook to the jaw that sent the Falangist sprawling on his ass on the sidewalk. The knife rolled on the pavement, the other two boys had second thoughts, they had suddenly lost their nerve. They looked at each other to see who would go first. Richard's left arm was bleeding, he had cut himself blocking the knife blow, the sharp blade had gone through his white shirt. The sleeve turned red and dripped down onto the ground. One of the young men picked up the knife off the floor while the other jumped on top of him grabbing his good arm. When he was about to stab him in the side, the deafening sound of a gunshot stopped him.

"Let's go, get out of here" - But the youths didn't move. - "Get the fuck out, damn it!"

He angrily yelled pointing his shotgun at the face of the one holding the knife. The two of them helped their partner up and ran off.

"Thanks, you saved my life." - Richard extended his hand to greet him, but Tomás pushed him, knocking him on his ass.

"Thanks? Go back to your damned country. What the hell are you doing here? I've got enough problems already without those Falangist sonsofbitches coming after me too."

The German spoke too loudly. They were still walking through narrow, dark alleyways.

"Shut up for once, you're going to attract everyone's attention. Go back to the mine, it's two or three hours walk, but you can't get lost, you'll make it no problem."

"No, I don't want to go back, I'm not part of that company. I'm staying here with you."

Tomás García Hernández pointed his shotgun at him, pressing the tip of the barrel to his chest.

"Get out of my sight or I'll shoot you right now." - He didn't hesitate.

The only light illuminating them was that of the stars. The Milky Way could be seen crossing from one end of the clear sky to the other. A shooting star crossed the sky. Tomás looked up and saw two shooting stars at once, crossing paths in the firmament. Then he lowered his shotgun. As if he had seen something inexplicable that suddenly made him change his mind.

"Alright, you'll come with me."

He slung the shotgun over his shoulder and put on his pince-nez glasses he took out of his jacket pocket. He was a handsome young man, his manner of dress, walking and speaking denoted he was no peasant. Well trimmed beard, short hair parted to one side. His hands were soft, with long slender fingers, well manicured nails. From all this Beckenbauer deduced he must be some kind of intellectual, one of the revolutionary leaders. It was odd, those who defended workers' rights were usually from the other class. Bourgeois kids and aristocrats looking for adventure, to change the world on a whim. They arrived at the back of a tavern, Tomás knocked three times on the door, heard the bolt slide, and they let them in. Inside was a group of armed Anarchists. Pepe Baena took his pistol from behind his waist, he wore it tucked between his back and the leather belt of his corduroy pants. One of the young men next to him also aimed his shotgun at the German.

"Put your weapons down!" - Tomás angrily yelled at them.

And he had to grab Baena by the neck, as he seemed determined to kill Richard before hearing or saying a word.

"You can't bring him here, he stinks like a German from a mile away."

The leader, Pepe, was very irritable. Since the death of his older brother at the hands of the police, he didn't trust anyone. He was of medium height, stocky with a brutish face, scowling, black beret pulled down to his eyebrows. He dressed like a peasant and his hands confirmed it.

"You're not the one giving orders here. If I brought him it's because I saw something. The council has to see him, after everyone talks we'll decide what to do with him."

They tied his hands behind his back, took him out through the courtyard and shoved him to another building.

Due to the harsh working conditions, sometimes inhumane, the miners formed protest groups carrying out major strikes and demonstrations nationwide. In some places there were even children working. The main cause of death was explosions and collapses caused by pockets of firedamp gas. Chastagnaret argued that despite the rise in gross wages in the late 19th century, the quality of life had declined due to the number of accidents and mortality in the villages where they lived. This was evidenced by the lack of schools and educational materials for children. Life expectancy in mining villages corroborated the worsening situation. At that time life expectancy was around thirty-seven, while in the mining villages of Cartagena it was around eighteen. Hard work and poor diet, compounded by air and water pollution, together proved a fatal combination.

Chapter 9

The Party Headquarters

DESPITE TOMÁS GARCÍA'S objections, they dragged him along, roughly. Baena had become an extremist and radical since what happened to his brother. Going from being a simple, quiet country man to an aggressive union revolutionary. So much so he had openly proposed in the party committee carrying out armed actions. They blindfolded him and walked until reaching the inside of a warehouse. The party leadership was gathered there. Elías, Tomás's father, had the floor. He was talking about agrarian reforms and day laborers' wages. He was one of the most respected leaders, an honorable man.

"What were you thinking? How did you get the idea to bring a Nazi here?" - Tomás's father said angrily when he saw a German there.

He was a chubby man, round face and broad nose. He and his wife made an odd couple, she was much taller, dark-skinned and thin.

"Father, you know I wouldn't have brought him without good reason. I was about to shoot him, but I saw him fight three Falangists. He's got guts."

"He's your father?" - And he turned to the man with his hand extended. "Pleased to meet you, your son saved my life."

Pepe Baena pushed him back to keep him from approaching Elías.

"What the fuck do you think this is?" - Baena raised his open hand intending to hit him.

"Alright, take it easy." - Tomás's father stopped him.

38

They were deciding what to do with him. Take him back safely to the mine or shoot him halfway leaving him dumped on the roadside. But before Elías made any statement or there was any kind of show of hands vote, Tomás said his mother should see him.

They were a unique community, with deeply ingrained ancient beliefs, superstition as the Falangists called it. But the community remained united: Tomás's mother had treated many of them, even saving their lives when they were children and their parents had no money to pay a doctor. She came from a family of Gypsies, seers and healers. She once helped a fifteen-year-old girl who had become very ill, managing to save her, but she lost the fetus, she was pregnant by the young master of the house where she worked. The Falangists had spread the rumor that she performed abortions.

Basilisa, La Basi, as friends called her, was half Gypsy, thin, dark skin, large dark eyes, long curly hair which at her age was streaked with gray. She took him by the hand as if he were someone she knew and led him to a nearby room so they could talk alone.

"Mother, be careful with the foreigner." - Her son had also seen something in his eyes.

She closed the door of the small room, where there was a round table and two wooden chairs with esparto seats. Behind her there was a kind of altar, a small plaster virgin illuminated by many candles.

"I'd like to read your hands and see what the cards say." - She asked his name.

"Richard Beckenbauer." - He didn't believe in that, but it made him nervous, he preferred not to know certain things, better not dwell on how and when he would die.

"What was your mother's full name, first and last?" - She stared intently into his eyes, as if she could see inside him.

"María Arjona Fábregas."

"She lived in Malaga before getting pregnant and leaving with that German."

"Did you know her?"

"My parents traveled the country, they were tinsmiths, making a living fixing pots and pans. I inherited the gift from my mother and my son has it too. Many people asked us for advice, we would read their hands and remove the evil eye curse. I remember your mother's case, she was just a girl when she got pregnant and before leaving Malaga she came to see me to ask me to tell her fortune.

As they spoke she took his hand and anointed his finger with oil, then let the drops fall into a glass of water to remove the evil eye curse.

"Why did you come to exploit the resources of our land?" - The question was direct.

"I'm not an engineer and I'm not the least bit interested in mining. I don't care for the Nazis or their damned ideas either. I'm a racecar driver, it's the only thing I know how to do, drive faster than anyone. But an unfortunate accident landed me in prison for attempting against Hitler. Although they found no evidence of it, they kept me locked up awaiting trial until they found a use for me. My brother was the engineer in charge of the mine. When he died... they thought maybe I could help them. Because of the language and the school thing."

The woman muttered a sort of prayer under her breath. Then she hugged him and they went back outside. The warehouse was now practically empty, Pepe Baena and his crew were gone. She approached her son and husband.

"Tomás, you'll be in charge of him. It won't be hard to confirm what he said. About the accident and if he really was in prison. And it would be best if you leave him at the German school tomorrow morning."

Tomás tried to argue something but his father didn't let him speak. He had been taught since he was a boy: you hunt it, you eat it.

Chapter 10

The Führer's Plan

WHEN DIANE KLUM AND engineer Horten arrived at the school early in the morning, Richard Beckenbauer was already there. Sitting on the teacher's desk, happily eating an apple like a child. His shirt was dirty with dried blood stains on the sleeve, but he was smiling as if he had won one of his races. He told them what had happened, his adventures, the little excursion to Almeria, the Falangists and also that he had befriended the leader Tomás García Hernández.

"I don't understand how you managed to contact the anarchists and they didn't shoot you dead." - commented the teacher laughing.

"A guy has his ways." - He bragged now.

"Well, Tomás is not the most influential person in the party, his father and mother call the shots, plus there's that Pepe Baena, the more radical youths are loyal to him." - Michael Horten seemed jealous, trying to downplay Richard's story.

"You're right, I've also met Elías García and his wife." - He paused pensively for a moment. "What's her name?"

"Basilisa Hernández."

"That's it, La Basi, she liked me, she even read my cards and gave me her blessing, I'm practically one of the family now."

He boasted in such a way that all three of them laughed.

"Alright crazy pilot, write up your report and take a shower because you smell like a bear."

He went up to the mine in the Opel Olympia, took a shower and then sat down in front of the huge Mercedes typewriter with clean clothes and a cup of coffee. He handed in his report and fell asleep on the bed. He had that old dream again where he was flying, that repetitive dream he used to have when he was bedridden in prison, only this time the images were clearer, sharper, he flew over the fields of Almeria. Someone knocked loudly on his room door. A soldier informed him that Commander Lindemann had summoned him.

In the meeting room amidst a cloud of smoke stood the commander in military at-ease position, legs shoulder-width apart, hands clasped behind his back, looking outside through the window glass. At the back, at a table, the little man with evil eyes was scrutinizing the documents in a folder.

"How did you manage to contact them? You know these people control the area, they have power over what happens in the mines. One word from them and all the miners will go on strike." - Commander Uli spoke casually, almost as if they were comrades.

"I told them about my accident and that I was in prison for a while. As soon as they confirm it, I'll be one of the group."

"Well done, son."

He put out the half-smoked cigarette he held between his fingers in a large glass ashtray full of butts, and spoke up. The mine manager had a wrinkled shirt, untucked and a crooked tie.

"Find out how we can sign the concession with these people. Because we built them a school and gave them medicine, but they still won't come to their senses."

"I'll see what I can do."

"Look!" - he showed him some plans. "We have direct orders from Hitler himself to expand the mine, we need to increase production."

It was an enormous project, they wanted to destroy a large part of the mountain range, open huge open-pit mines and would need thousands of workers. They wanted to gut their land while at the same time using them as cheap labor. The man definitely didn't seem to be in his right mind, he thought to himself.

"And if they don't grant us the rights? Maybe they have ideals, they're not motivated by money." - Now the conversation had become serious.

"The other option is to help the Falangists. If they take power everything will be solved. Of course we can't start a civil war, it would be badly viewed by the international community." They were still under the watchful eye of the French and British. It wasn't just about this one mine, there were several throughout the country, it was about securing resources, resources needed for what was coming.

At that moment Richard didn't understand what he was referring to, Hitler's expansionist plans. He mulled it over, but didn't quite grasp what the mine manager had meant. What was looming? He was starting to sense something, he wasn't naïve, the large quantities of tungsten extracted in Spain and exported to Germany, what the pilot Christoph Schneider said about how easily civilian passenger planes could be converted into military bombers. But who would they fight against? Who would they declare war on? The Russians, the French or the British? None of it sounded logical. The commander spoke again:

"Son, you have four months to gain their trust, to get them to grant us all mining rights. Once that avenue is exhausted, we'll find another way, alliances are already being forged with top commanders of the Spanish army."

They made it clear to him that one way or another, they would take control of the mines in Spain. But reaching an armed conflict seemed like too much. Was that mineral so important?

Chapter 11

Party

THE TEACHER SHOWED him documents with photos and names of the anarchist leaders, quizzing him to check what he knew, who they were, the authority they held and who he shouldn't get too close to. She showed him the photo of the leader, the surly young man.

"HIS NAME IS JOSÉ LUÍS Baena, Pepe Baena, and soon he will hold command of the entire party in Almeria." - Diane explained.

"Yes, I don't like that guy at all. They told me he lost a brother and he's a little touched in the head."

"That's why I'm telling you, stay as far from him as you can."

She also talked about Tomás García Hernández:

"Writer and pilot, he's one of the most renowned intellectuals in the area, and in this city all the workers do what his father says. He decides whether or not they come work at the mine. Despite his easygoing appearance, he is extremely intelligent, don't be fooled by appearances, Tomás's grandfather, Elías's father, is one of the most important landowners in Andalusia. I guess he's suffered the greatest misfortune, being capitalists and having an anarchist son and grandson."

They went back down to Rodalquilar, this time Diane rode with them in the Opel and told Michael to drive, she didn't want any shocks. She kept talking to Richard about the political situation in the area. The conflict between leftist and rightist parties. The situation had become so entrenched that neither side could stand the sight of the other. No one respected the ideas of those in front. The hatred between them had reached such a point that the situation could blow up at any time.

"What a mess, you have no idea what an anarchist, unionist, communist or Falangist is." - Michael blurted it out in envy, now they treated Richard like the darling.

"I may not know anything about politics, but on the first day I befriended the boss's son." - And he winkilyed at him with disdain.

Tomás García greeted him and invited him to go with them, they had planned a small trip to Huelva, to a festival held in the town of Almonte. They took off in an old black matte four-door Renault Vivasix, it was almost square like a box, the next model, the Vivastella looked nothing like it, more rounded with smooth, harmonious lines.

They arrived in Almonte, Huelva. In the marshlands, they were celebrating the festival of La Saca de las yeguas. The celebration consists of gathering the wild horses from the mountains and marshes, about fourteen herds of over six hundred heads. They are brought down to the village, put into a kind of bullring for the mares to be shaved, branded and shod. No ropes or sticks are used, it's about the men's skill to get the horses under control with their bare hands. The German was surprised, festivals in Spain were primitive and violent, people risked their lives the same before a wild colt or a fighting bull. Although first they always prayed to the patron saint - in this case San Pedro - so that no tragedy would occur. Of course, upon taking part he began to understand it, not with brain logic, it was something more visceral, ancestral sensations and memories imprinted in our DNA. Running down the mountain guiding the horses to the village, the shouts, the adrenaline, the excitement and also the courage given by the manzanilla wine or Brandy de Jerez. In ancient times this celebration was the symbolic initiation into manhood. Catching a horse for the first time and guiding it to the village. The ancient festival was regulated in 1504 by an ordinance of the Duke of Medina Sidonia. The herders gather the horses from different areas of the Doñana marshlands: La Marismilla, Las Nuevas, Rincón del Pescador, Vuelta de la Madre, Matasgorda, El Lobo, Las Mogeas and Lucio de las Yeguas, rounding them up on the beach in front of El Rocío, heading towards Almonte.

The real reason Tomás García and Pepe Baena were there was to negotiate in secret with leaders of other leftist groups, to organize themselves covertly. Doing it at a festival in plain sight was the best way not to draw attention.

"Richard come here." - With the help of a boy, Tomás held a colt by the forelock. "Come on, get on, show us what Germans are made of."

Beckenbauer had never ridden a horse in his life, his thing was motorized transport, cars and motorcycles. He approached the animal and when he placed his hand on the croup, it stirred, baring its teeth, neighing and rearing up. That's when he felt his pulse quicken, getting on a wild five hundred kilo beast was no game. He looked at Pepe Baena who wouldn't stop laughing. It could be one of his tricks to get rid of him. Riling up the horse so there would be an accident. But Tomás's gaze conveyed trust.

"I've never ridden before."

"So big and so cowardly." - Baena said laughing.

"Take it easy, first put your hand on his muzzle, let him see what you're doing, let the animal trust you. He can feel your fear, you have to convey calm and serenity."

He carefully mounted, trying to remain calm, but the horse started moving nervously. Tomás let go and the animal bolted. The German lasted three seconds on top before he was rolling on the ground. He got up brushing the dust off his pants.

"Now Tomás was laughing too."

Pepe Baena furiously mounted his colt, kicking and punching managed to subdue the animal.

"Fancy German gentleman, don't be so posh. You're out of place at this festival." - Baena always seemed to be in a bad mood, angry at the whole world.

But Richard didn't give up and tried it once more, now his attitude had changed, his gaze was that of a race car driver. He mounted decisively and when the colt tried to throw him off again he showed no fear and the animal noticed it. He rode swiftly as the wind, quickly catching up to Baena. He brushed past him at full speed.

"You Germans are all crazy." - He shouted.

Now it was Richard who laughed.

The party continued at night, music of guitars, handclaps and pretty girls with polka dot dresses, swirling their wide flounces as they danced. They visited several taverns, after drinking quite a bit Tomás recited some of his poems and the spontaneous audience broke into applause. Beckenbauer realized he was a charismatic man, an intellectual close to the people. Who fought as hard as anyone, but also knew how to drink and have fun. At dawn they staggered arm in arm through the streets of Huelva, both had drunk too much, the German had a bottle of wine in his hand. They sang out of tune.

"Quiet, sleep off your drunkenness!" - yelled a fat woman dressed in mourning, leaning out the window of a small balcony full of geraniums.

"Shhh!" - The German hushed, holding his index finger to his lips. When he turned he lost his balance and both tumbled to the ground. The bottle shattered.

They laughed for a while, then Tomás took a crooked cigarette from his pocket and tried to light it with a match, but he was too drunk to manage it.

"I knew your brother." - Tomás told him, his tone and expression melancholy. "I don't know what they told you, but he wasn't on the Nazi side, he was a good man, that's why they killed him."

He implied they had told Richard a bunch of lies. He had become a nuisance to the Nazis and they were the ones who killed him. Richard Beckenbauer began to entertain the possibility that it might be true, that his brother had been murdered by the Nazis.

José Luís Baena pulled up in the old Renault Vivasix and stopped in the middle of the street. He got out and helped them into the back seat.

"Come on, we've got a long way to go, you can sleep in the car."

They set off on a trip with stops in Extremadura, Galicia, Asturias and Bilbao ending in Pamplona. They toured all the mining basins, the tungsten and coal exploitations. They were preparing a rebellion, a revolutionary strike with armed miners wielding dynamite and shotguns.

There was a strong labor movement in the mining basins, where the CNT's influence was noticeable. From the region of Siruela it extended over a large area, from Cabeza de Buey to the limits of Cáceres and Toledo, reaching the mines of Almadén. The unions from different regions joined together in Andalusia and Extremadura. With General Primo de Rivera's dictatorship the anarcho-syndicalists lost part of their influence and organizational structure when declared illegal at the central headquarters. Said prohibition forced them underground. Some grouped around other legal associations such as the UGT in order to remain active. After the fall of the dictatorship they quickly reorganized. The southern Badajoz area saw extensive activity. In Cáceres province the CNT's authority spread from Navalmoral de la Mata to Jarandilla, Peraleda de la Mata, Hervás, Aldeanueva del Camino, Oliva de Plasencia, Talayuela, Pasarón de la Vera, Valdehúncar and other towns. CNT unions developed in Jerez de los Caballeros, Fregenal de la Sierra, Fuente de Cantos, Bienvenida, Usagre, Llerena,

Campillo de Llerena, Guareña, Quintana, Berlanga, Malpartida de la Serena, Malcocinado, Don Benito, Villanueva de la Serena, Mérida. Richard Beckenbauer was finding out about the real situation of workers throughout the country.

"The German money used for tungsten extraction at O Fontao attracted many laborers and also the most expensive whores in the country." - commented Baena.

The Galician mines were first exploited by the English and French for tin, tungsten had no value until the Germans and Americans became interested in it. The only one sleeping warm was the mine manager, who had a nice house, the miners lived in barracks. Many workers suffered fatal falls down the shafts. Deaths from work accidents were very common. The manager of the Almeria mines and Commander Uli Lindemann had control over all the tungsten extracted in Spain. Both took frequent trips, business visits to see how things were going, for that purpose they had the Junkers plane.

In Asturias after the revolutionary general strike of 1934, many union leaders had been shot, the rest were in prison, but they had relatives on the outside who kept them informed. The entire movement was underground, Tomás García and Pepe Baena were calling for reorganization. New times were expected, the 1936 elections were around the corner and winds of change were felt.

The festivals began with the traditional chupinazo rocket launch from the town hall balcony. The square was packed with people singing and shouting.

General Mola had met during the San Fermin festivities with the other generals who were preparing the uprising, the coup d'etat. Both sides seemed to be gearing up for possible armed action.

"What do you think, Beckenbauer? These aren't horses." - He pointed to the bulls running down Estafeta Street.

"I think you Spaniards aren't right in the head." - But what was wrong with these people, they seemed impatient to die. Wild horses are one thing, bulls another, a bullfighter is one thing, ordinary people running in front of a herd is another. The bullfighter is a professional and knows what he's doing, that's how he earns his bread, but what need does ordinary people have to stand in front of a horned beast? He wondered as he watched the young men run by.

"It's not about believing or thinking, it's about acting, you have to stand in front to know how it feels." - Tomás's poetic answers didn't convince him.

"You're not thinking of standing in front of them?"

"Thinking of it? Today don't drink too much because tomorrow the three of us are running." - Baena laughed before taking a swig from the wineskin.

"Don't count on me." - The German replied.

"Suit yourself, start walking back to Almeria now because pussies don't ride in my car." - He was about to take another drink when Richard snatched the wineskin from his hands and drank long.

"Looks like the little blondie's got balls." - Pepe punched him in the chest in greeting as Richard drank from the wineskin.

Tomás already knew it, he had seen it with his own eyes fighting the three Falangists and not backing down even when the knife wounded his forearm.

They went to the plaza to watch the bullfight and sat next to an American writer and journalist, one Ernest Hemingway. Beckenbauer respected the courage of the bullfighters, but it seemed to him a brutal, primitive, bloody festival. Despite its beauty he considered it unnecessary to cause suffering to such a brave and noble animal. Spain was and is an ancient country, with traditions dating back beyond the Middle Ages. The San Fermin festivities originated in the combination of three festivals, the liturgical events in honor of San Fermin prior to the 12th century, the trade markets and the bullfights documented since the 14th century. Ernest Hemingway helped make the San Fermins an internationally known festival, basing his novel The Sun

Also Rises on the celebrations. Nearly a million people attend Pamplona every year.

"Do as Esteban says, she's from Pamplona and has been running from the bulls all her life." - Tomás advised him.

After commending themselves to the saint they got ready to run with the bulls. As soon as they saw the beasts everyone started running like crazy. The first pileups, shoving and falls occurred, the bulls getting closer to them. The four of them ran side by side, barely two meters from the horns of the lead animal.

"Get out of the way German, the bull's gonna get you!" - Baena pushed him aside.

His heart was pounding so hard it felt like it would come out of his chest. He had a similar sensation to what he felt when his car exploded, right before crashing into the grandstand. Time seemed to stop as he lost his balance and fell to the side. He felt the animal's horn brush his back. Then he rolled on the ground and the rest of the herd trampled over him. He got some kicks but nothing serious. During that whole time there had been silence, now the screams of the people deafened him. When he got up he saw the bull hook Pepe at the Estafeta curve, launching him through the air as if he were a rag doll. Tomás and Esteban managed to jump aside. It had all happened in an instant, in the blink of an eye. Nothing like what you saw from the other side of the barrier. Baena lay still on the ground and Richard thought his time had come. That was it. José Luís Baena's stupid way to die. The German ran towards them to see how serious the goring had been. Baena got up with his shirt in tatters, a broken tooth and blood in his mouth.

"Did you see it? Did you see it German? I touched the bull." - He shouted euphorically.

The others also shouted with him, releasing all the pent-up adrenaline.

"Come on, let's eat something because I'm starving." - Baena said as they hugged greeting each other.

"A drink for the brave!" - A man on the other side of the barrier shouted, offering Pepe Baena his wineskin.

They felt more alive than ever, charged with youth and energy. They went from celebration to celebration throughout the day, recounting their adventure over and over. Each one from their unique point of view, how they had seen death up close and how Baena had flown through the air. He laughed now missing a tooth. Battle scars he called them, memories that I have lived.

Ten days later he sat in front of the Mercedes typewriter typing up his report. He found out quite a bit, the preparations the anarchists were making throughout the country. How the more extreme groups were arming themselves. He understood they planned to carry out attacks against Falangist leaders. This infuriated the commander, the continual riots were wearing out his patience. Diane Klum went to speak with him.

"Now more than ever, we have to redouble our efforts, we have more and more children at school every day." - Diane wanted to open two more classrooms. The children were making great progress.

At school they were given uniforms and three meals a day. The older ones already knew how to read.

"Do you really think we care about those people?" - Commander Uli Lindemann was very unhappy about Beckenbauer's report. "Our country and us as loyal servants of the fatherland, should only care about getting that damned ore. Don't forget we're here temporarily, defending the Führer's interests. When our mission ends we'll go back home and no one will remember these wretches."

The teacher thought there was still some humanity left in the commander or the mine manager, but that wasn't the case, they had become radicalized, turning into real Nazis. They didn't care about the population, not even the school kids, the only thing they pursued was moving up the National Socialist hierarchy. To go home hands full even if it meant many miners dying in misery.

Chapter 12

Flight at Dusk

TOMÁS TOOK HIM TO THE airfield, he hadn't talked about his other passion until then, he knew his side as a writer, but didn't know anything about his hundreds of flight hours training as an aerobatic pilot. The aerodrome was located on a clay plain. The yellow earth rose into the air stirred up by the propellers. At the back of a hangar he kept his small plane. It was an old Bristol F 2B that served in the British Royal Air Force in World War I and about sixteen aircraft operated in the Morocco conflict in Spain, a total of sixty-four planes had ended their operational life just a few years ago. Pulling some strings he got one for scrap price. Now reconverted as a civilian recreational aircraft. Tomás used the biplane to train as an aerobatic pilot. It still retained its green paint. It had an Hispano Suiza eight-cylinder three hundred horsepower engine. Of course it had been demilitarized, the 7.7 mm Vickers machine gun and two rear Lewis guns had been removed along with the Scarff ring mount.

"Here's my pretty girl Bris." - He stroked the fuselage. "Bris, Richard, Richard Bris..."

He made a formal introduction, as if it were a person. In the German's eyes it didn't look like much, an old tin can with wings. After a visual check they wheeled it outside. It was a splendid day, blue sky with some fluffy white clouds and a gentle breeze.

"This is not a race car, but if you treat it the same way, with care, fear and respect, it will make you feel free. True and real freedom, being above the world, able to go wherever you want." - Now the poet Tomás spoke, with his heart and not his head. "To be an aerobatic pilot you have to trust your plane, be one with the machine."

"Even though I would never have used your words, I understand you perfectly. In a race, you also entrust your life to the machine in a way."

"Of course you Germans aren't known for expressing your feelings." - He pointed it out with such grace and charm that they both laughed.

Beckenbauer rode in the co-pilot's seat. Tomás tested the engine with a few revs, then they taxied to the runway threshold. They lined up into the wind and started the takeoff run. The German was surprised when he felt himself in the air, for such an old jalopy it had taken off in just a few meters. The sensations were different from the Junkers, he felt the rapid climb as if his stomach had been left on the ground.

"How was breakfast?" - Tomás yelled at him, they had no intercom and the engine noise was deafening.

"All good, so far the coffee is still in place."

He pulled the stick to his chest and chopped the throttle, the Bristol's nose pointed skyward for a few seconds, as long as it took to lose lift and fall into a dive. The negative G forces were harder to take, something he wasn't used to. In his single seater the forces were always positive, only when the wheels lifted off the ground did he feel something similar, but it was nothing like this.

"How about some barrels?" - He motioned the maneuver with his hand.

"Go for it, go for it, don't be shy!" - Although he was starting to feel queasy.

The abrupt changes in direction produced a strange sensation, going from positive to negative forces in a sustained series made him feel very fragile. The heavy body stuck to the seat and the next instant weightless, holding on not to fly out of the plane. The blood rushed to his feet and he felt like passing out. When Tomás saw the German's pale face, he quit the aerobatics and flew steadily along the coast.

"Much better, I prefer sightseeing." - Richard joked. "I'll get you for this, someday I'll take you for a ride in a real car."

"What's that?"

"Nothing, nothing, better you not know."

The scenery was wonderful, the mountain ranges, the jagged cliffs in bizarre shapes and the blue of the sky merging into infinity with the other darker blue of the sea. He leveled the plane and let it cruise.

"Take the controls!" - He yelled.

At first he did so fearfully, then feeling how the Bristol faithfully responded to his commands, he began guiding it from side to side. The sensation was fantastic, like suddenly taking the reins of his life, holding the world in his hands or rather at his feet. Up there nothing that happened on the ground mattered. Even someone as powerful as Commander Uli Lindemann was no more than a small ant from up there.

"Look!" - He pointed to the lighthouse on the cliffs overlooking a bay.

"That's Portmán!" - He pointed out the mining area.

The damage was incredible, much greater than what he had seen in Rodalquilar. Here the bowels of the earth were spilled out, strewn in intensely colored rivers and meanders. Sulfur, iron oxide, lead and mercury.

"Check it out!" - He pointed to the compass that had gone crazy. The heavy metal accumulation was so intense it confused the indicator making it spin in circles.

They say the ancients dedicated the seventh day to giving thanks to the sun and that spring Sunday it shone brightly. The airshow was held the first weekend of each month. With good weather the stands were packed. In all directions cereal fields extended as far as the eye could see; green fields, red with poppies and white with daisies. As if they had been planted for the occasion, each plot of land was dominated by one species. The airport's central runway was narrow and paved, the grass sidelines were used by lighter aircraft. While children ran and played around the stands, parents lined up near the hangars, where there was a stall with marinated shark and fried fish. For sure most of the kids came to see the planes and most parents came for the food and drink. Accompanying the fried food cones with craft beer bottles or natural fruit slushies.

First the oldest planes went out, followed gradually by more modern, advanced models. Those old piston engine planes powered by propellers captivated the hearts of attendees. Each one had its own particular charm, the sound of its engines, its shapes and its flight. I suppose the kind of mystical magic felt by the first people who saw them fly is still latent in their engines, captivating people who watch them today in the same way.

He looked at planes as if they were living beings, pampering them and even sometimes talking to them. Once he told Richard:

"It's amazing, but here" - Tomás pointed to the large mine crater - "there used to be centuries-old trees, especially holm oaks, so old that it's possible the ancient Roman legions rested under them. The Germans destroyed it all in two days."

Richard realized he hadn't said "you Germans", he had differentiated between him and the rest of his countrymen, speaking to him as if he were Spanish too.

They spent the day at the airfield, after flying Tomás started checking the engine, dismantling it almost completely. Richard also got his hands dirty with grease, he was in his element, he loved taking engines apart and putting them back together and a Hispano Suiza was something special. They finished at nightfall, lit by a portable electric lamp. On the way back home along the beach road Tomás took off his clothes and ran naked into the water. It was a warm night, lit by an almost full moon.

"Come on, it won't shrink!" - He gestured with his arms for Richard to get in.

Beckenbauer didn't think twice, took off his shirt, pants, underwear and shoes and ran naked across the beach until the water reached his knees, then he dove in headfirst. It was freezing.

"Well it seems I have shrunk. Damn, it's cold!"

He slowly approached Tomás almost inconspicuously and suddenly grabbed him by the neck, dunking him underwater.

"This is war. Spain against Germany." - He shouted as they played fighting trying to dunk each other.

"Two-nil! Do you give up?"

"Not a chance, now you'll see..." - And they kept wrestling like children until they were frozen stiff.

They came out naked onto the beach and had to jog on the spot to warm up. Then they lay on their clothes, listening to the sound of the sea and looking at the starry sky. Sitting in the sand Tomás broke into reciting some poetry from memory, García Lorca, Machado and Miguel Hernández. Staring into the starry infinity.

"My mother believes in supernatural forces, that almost no one can see. She says I'm special." - He spoke staring intently at the stars.

"And she's right, you're crazy as a loon." - The German laughed.

"Well, she says you have a gift. You're special too." - Now he stared intently into Richard's eyes.

"Maybe we're both crazy." - He returned the gaze.

He realized that he often stares at Tomás enthralled, especially when he speaks from the heart in his political speeches, but also when he listens to him reading his poems aloud. Tomás García Hernández had a special air and he noticed it. He had seen many people at car races, nouveau riche trying to feign manners they didn't really possess; Tomás was the opposite, dressed simply but oozing education and culture through every pore. Just watching him sit, walk or say anything, he seemed surrounded by a halo of light. The physical beauty of the ballet dancer, the strength of the revolutionary who guides the masses with his words, the precise words of a poem. Richard Beckenbauer felt insignificant like a grain of sand on the beach and at the same time alive and happy like when he was a child, enjoying every moment without thinking about tomorrow. His life in Berlin was so different he could never have imagined living like this. It wasn't about money or luxuries, they usually walked everywhere, hiking from village to village, that was part of the charm. The simplicity of finding happiness in little things, despite the misfortunes and misery surrounding them. Finding the solidarity of ordinary people who shared what little they had with them, porridge, breadcrumbs, rice and wine. Despite the extreme poverty there was always a reason to celebrate: a birthday, a baptism or a wedding. Spain was a country of contrasts, but all of them from one end to the other, Andalusians, Extremadurans, Galicians, Catalans, Basques, all shared that lust for life not seen elsewhere.

Chapter 13

The Poet

"WHAT THE HELL'S THE matter with you, kid? I thought we understood each other." - Commander Lindemann was quite angry. Truthfully, I don't recall ever seeing him laugh.

He asked Richard to prepare a report immediately, it had been over twenty days since he submitted one. As soon as the meeting with the commander ended, he immediately started typing up his report on the Mercedes typewriter. He had doubts about recounting everything he was finding out, so he decided not to go into details. He was losing his identity or finding a new one. He no longer felt German, he felt comfortable in Spain, becoming part of its people. He remembered what Tomás told him that drunken night, that his brother hadn't been killed by anti-patriots and much less was it a matter of chance. The Nazis themselves got him out of the way, either because he no longer followed orders or perhaps because he knew too much and had become a danger to them. Tomás also talked about the start of the war, first here in Spain and surely after in Europe, spreading like cancer throughout the world. The revenge of a frustrated corporal for having lost the First World War.

Michael Horten seemed closer, more of a friend, as if he could see that something was changing inside Richard. An inner change in the way of thinking and acting, reflected in his attitude. Now he trusted him more and was gradually letting out little things, implying he didn't work for the Nazis. Until one day he confessed his grandfather was Jewish.

He saw with his own eyes the struggle of the anarchists and unionists. Their noble ideals. How the community helped each other. And also the respect not only for people, but for animals and nature too.

One day Tomás had told him:

"It's unbelievable, but here" - Tomás pointed to the large mine crater - "there were centuries-old trees, especially holm oaks, so old that the ancient Roman legions may have rested under them. The Germans destroyed it all in two days."

Richard realized he hadn't said "you Germans", he had differentiated between him and the rest of his countrymen, speaking to him as if he were Spanish too.

They spent the day at the airfield, after flying Tomás started checking the engine, dismantling it almost completely. Richard also got his hands dirty with grease, he was in his element, he loved taking engines apart and putting them back together and an Hispano Suiza was something special. They finished at nightfall, lit by a portable electric lamp. On the way back home along the beach road Tomás took off his clothes and ran naked into the water. It was a warm night, lit by an almost full moon.

"Come on, it won't shrink!" - He gestured with his arms for Richard to get in.

Beckenbauer didn't think twice, took off his shirt, pants, underwear and shoes and ran naked across the beach until the water reached his knees, then he dove in headfirst. It was freezing.

"Well it seems I have shrunk. Damn, it's cold!"

He slowly approached Tomás almost inconspicuously and suddenly grabbed him by the neck, dunking him underwater.

"This is war. Spain against Germany." - He shouted as they played fighting trying to dunk each other.

"Two-nil! Do you give up?"

"Not a chance, now you'll see..." - And they kept wrestling like children until they were frozen stiff.

They came out naked onto the beach and had to jog on the spot to warm up. Then they lay on their clothes, listening to the sound of the sea and looking at the starry sky. Sitting in the sand Tomás broke into reciting some poetry from memory, García Lorca, Machado and Miguel Hernández. Staring into the starry infinity.

"My mother believes in supernatural forces, that almost no one can see. She says I'm special." - He spoke staring intently at the stars.

"And she's right, you're crazy as a loon." - The German laughed.

"Well, she says you have a gift. You're special too." - Now he stared intently into Richard's eyes.

"Maybe we're both crazy." - He returned the gaze.

He realized that he often stares at Tomás enthralled, especially when he speaks from the heart in his political speeches, but also when he listens to him reading his poems aloud. Tomás García Hernández had a special air and he noticed it. He had seen many people at car races, nouveau riche trying to feign manners they didn't really possess; Tomás was the opposite, dressed simply but oozing education and culture through every pore. Just watching him sit, walk or say anything, he seemed surrounded by a halo of light. The physical beauty of the ballet dancer, the strength of the revolutionary who guides the masses with his words, the precise words of a poem. Richard Beckenbauer felt insignificant like a grain of sand on the beach and at the same time alive and happy like when he was a child, enjoying every moment without thinking about tomorrow. His life in Berlin was so different he could never have imagined living like this. It wasn't about money or luxuries, they usually walked everywhere, hiking from village to village, that was part of the charm. The simplicity of finding happiness in little things, despite the misfortunes and misery surrounding them. Finding the solidarity of ordinary people who shared what little they had with them, porridge, breadcrumbs, rice and wine. Despite the extreme poverty there was always a reason to celebrate: a birthday, a baptism or a wedding. Spain was a country of contrasts, but all of them from one end to the other, Andalusians, Extremadurans, Galicians, Catalans, Basques, all shared that lust for life not seen elsewhere.

When he walked into the school he came face to face with Professor Diane Klum, who was surprised. Not only because of how long it had been since she saw him, but also because of how much he had changed physically. From the color of his hair and eyes, now lighter, to his vital, energetic appearance, although he was quite thinner.

"You don't look German anymore, you're very tanned and thin."

"Yes, we spend a lot of time walking back and forth from village to village, to talk to the workers."

"Well, you have to eat more meat or wear baggier clothes, something that allows me to see you when you're sideways." - Diane joked.

"Why don't the kids want to go to school?"

"They're scared, especially their parents. At first the mining company decided to separate them from their families, make the school a boarding school. Parents could only come visit on Sundays. They intended to indoctrinate the children in Nazi ideology." - She recounted it with sincere sadness. "Some parents realized what was happening and started strikes and pickets. It got pretty ugly. You can't even imagine. The Spanish army even had to intervene. There were casualties in the clashes and union leaders were jailed."

"I'm more and more confused." - He confessed to the doctor.

"You're not the only one, I came here to help and I think we're doing more harm than good."

They were starting to trust each other, but they couldn't speak openly, not in that place.

"It would be better if we went for a walk." - Diane suggested.

They walked around the village of Rodalquilar, hiked down to the Las Negras beach and talked at length. Diane knew the plans the mine manager had in broad terms and the measures Commander Uli Lindemann was about to take.

"If you really care for these people, it's best not to give too many details in your reports. Things seem about to blow up. Leaders across the world, especially in Europe, seem to have lost their minds, common sense."

"True, while people here in Spain are having a hard time, they look the other way."

"Not only that, they're contributing to the disaster. They seem eager to see blood."

"You may be right, we've always envied them, all Europeans are jealous of them, because they have something we can't buy, we can't import." - Diane pointed at the sky with her palm.

Chapter 14

The Pilot

THEY MET AT THE AIRFIELD, where Tomás was waiting for him, preparing the old and pampered Bris. But Pepe Baena and two other young men, followers of his party, were there too. More than comrades, they looked like his lackeys.

"Look who we have here. The crazy German." That was the reception Pepe gave him.

The truth is, Richard was already used to his unpleasant jokes and bad mood. They had the plane outside, prepared for takeoff.

"Don't tell me you're teaching the Nazi to fly?" Pepe reprimanded Tomás.

"Baena, why don't you go for a walk with your boys."

"There, you even protect him, as if he were your girlfriend. Besides, we are dedicated to serious things, strolling is your thing."

"I remind you that the one who spends the nights drinking and the mornings sleeping off the binge is you." Beckenbauer intervened.

"Come on, don't mess with me, don't give me that now." He had touched a nerve. "Let there be peace."

They took off and did racetrack patterns, making low passes over the runway. After a few laps they landed and without stopping the engine Tomás got out of the Bristol.

"Don't worry, you're ready, do what I taught you, plus Bris will take care of you." Tomás yelled out instructions.

The expression on Pepe Baena's face, who was watching a few meters behind, was a mixture of surprise, envy and bitterness. He held a grudge against the Germans and they still didn't trust him.

"Do you want to see a dead German?" Baena laughed sarcastically, looking at the two young men accompanying him. "That idiot doesn't know how to fly."

The takeoff was somewhat rocky. He lifted the nose before gaining enough speed and the plane bounced back down with a thud before taking off after the rebound. Then he gained altitude, but had the left wing slightly lowered, flying the crooked Bristol, skidding in drift. Then he rectified, made a pass sticking the low pass on the runway at exactly one meter high.

"What do you have to say now?" He asked Pepe. "And he only has three hours of flight."

Pepe Baena's companions waved as they saw him pass over the runway. One whistled, bringing index finger and thumb to his mouth.

"Shut up you bunch of idiots." Pepe felt displaced. As if the German diminished his authority.

The impressions Richard had were hard to explain. Flying alone was something special, especially the first time. The feeling of freedom, of having control over his own life. A feeling of euphoria that turned into tension when it came time to land. He made a long approach to the runway, descending too soon over the cereal fields. So low that he could almost touch the ears with his hands. In the distance Tomás signaled him to gain altitude and that's when he noticed the fence in front of him. A slight movement of the stick and the plane made a small leap, clearing the fence by a few centimeters. Then he made a perfect landing. It seemed he had chosen the wrong profession, he was born to fly planes. He turned off the ignition and shut down the engine, got out of the Bristol and while Baena muttered unintelligible words between his teeth, the two young men accompanying him congratulated him.

He was startled to suddenly feel cold, Tomás had positioned himself behind him and poured a bucket of water over his head.

"PILOT BECKENBAUER YOU are hereby baptized." Now even the surly Pepe Baena laughed.

It was a whole tradition, baptizing new pilots with a bucket of cold water poured on them by surprise.

The next day Tomás was waiting for him again at the airfield, to continue his training, he wanted to teach him to really fly. But he was running late, which was not normal for the German. He had his beloved Bris in the middle of the runway, as the airfield was closed. Then he saw the unmistakable silhouette of a German-made Bücker Bü 131 Jungmann appear on the horizon. Before being able to remove his plane from the runway, the Jungmann's pilot performed the approach maneuver and jumping over it landed on the other side.

"What's wrong with him, didn't he see me?" Tomás approached with foul words. "You almost killed me, fucking lunatic."

And as he got closer the figure became more and more familiar, until he recognized the blue and clear gaze behind the aviator's goggles.

"What the hell! You bastard!" He hugged Beckenbauer. "Where did you get this beauty?"

"She's mine."

"Are you kidding?"

He had come to an agreement with Christoph, the mine pilot. Since he didn't use it much, it occurred to him that maybe they could share it, of course putting in his part, buying fifty percent of the plane. The Bü 131 Jungmann was a trainer aircraft used by the Luftwaffe, designed by Carl Bücker for SAAB. It was a sturdy and agile biplane with swept wings.

Now they could both fly in their own planes and perform aerobatic maneuvers as a group. They performed different maneuvers that they planned on the ground beforehand, rolling movements tilting the aircraft on its longitudinal axis and pitching on its vertical axis. They talked on the ground and took notes, their open palms simulated the planes explaining each of the aerobatics they had performed. Since they didn't have radio, they had to coordinate visually. The German knew many stories of racing pilots, but was completely oblivious to aviation aces. Tomás told him about the pioneers, the Wright brothers, Wilbur and Orville, Charles Lindbergh and Amelia Earhart. Also about Spanish aviation: the Plus Ultra flight and Juan de la Cierva's autogyro. Among all those famous aviators was his own uncle, his father's brother. Elías did not speak to them, his grandfather was a millionaire landowner, and when he saw that his own son had become a union leader he disinherited him.

"Although by the time that happened, my father had left home long ago. They had grown so far apart ideologically that they even stopped speaking."

Now he could imagine where that air of an English gentleman came from. They kept their wealthy upbringing almost secret. That they came from a well-off family. Almost every day they met at the airfield, Beckenbauer didn't know it, but without realizing it he was training for the Civil War, to fight in the air against Spanish Falangists, Italian Fascists and his own countrymen turned Nazis. One of those days, Tomás proposed a route, tracing it on the map, taking into account the fuel, the cruising speed of their planes and the wind drift, a well-calculated flight plan. Tomás García wanted to get close to Mallorca, to confirm secret information. He was told that Italian and German warships were supposedly maneuvering in Spanish waters. They spotted a tiny Nazi destroyer, trying to remain hidden near a small island. When they turned around they found themselves under fire from an Italian military plane. It was a Fiat CR 32 nicknamed

Chirri, manufactured in Italy. The fighter's engine doubled their power, it had almost twice as many horses and was armed with two 7.7 mm Breda-SAFAT machine guns, while they had nothing to defend themselves with, the only thing they could do was put all their skills into practice to try to throw it off. They quickly crossed each other in flight, always placing themselves behind the CR Fiat, no matter how much it fired it couldn't reach them. The tracer bullets shone like neon lights in the dark purple evening sky. It had Tomás' Bristol in sight, they couldn't shake it off them. He had to think of something, and fast. The fascist pilot fired a new burst of lead. Two bullets pierced the lower right wing of the old Brice. If they kept this up it would end up shooting them down. Richard thought:

— Either we both go down or neither of us does. —

He dove at the fighter and hit its tail with his landing gear, damaging the rudder. Now it could hardly maneuver and had to return to base.

The sturdy landing gear of the Bücker showed no damage, he was able to land without incident. The first thing Tomás did as soon as he got out of his plane was to hug the German.

"That was too close this time." Tomás couldn't believe they'd made it. "If you hadn't hit the rudder it would have killed us."

"Let's go for some beers, we've earned them." Richard proposed, making a mocking gesture as if yielding the right of way to an eminence.

Tomás jumped on his back, climbing up, he still couldn't believe they were alive.

"The Beckenbauer maneuver." He laughed out loud.

"Did you see the pilot's face? His eyes almost popped out of their sockets. He thought he was shooting ducks and the poor chicken was quite surprised when I rammed him."

"That guy will definitely need more than water to clean his seat."

"Yes, he probably shit his pants."

They didn't stop laughing and joking all the way back to Almería.

Chapter 15

A Gypsy Wedding

HE FELT LIKE A DIFFERENT person, even the memories of his life in Berlin had become hazy, blurred and faded, as if they weren't his. He had the feeling he had always lived in Almería, Tomás's life stories, the memories of playing in the fig tree in his orchard as a child, he had made them his own. He spent weeks away from the mine and when he returned to his room, he felt like a stranger. German magazines and newspapers seemed to be from another world. A distant world he wanted to know nothing about.

The commander summoned him once again. He appeared before him reluctantly, that man no longer had any kind of authority over his life.

"What happened, boy? You haven't sent any reports for three weeks." He no longer spoke like a father. He wore a military uniform and stood close to him. "I have doubts, it seems you have forgotten your duties. The time has come to return to Berlin."

"But I haven't finished the mission yet, I'm close to achieving it."

"You're wrong, kid. You've given me everything I need: names, addresses, rank and role in the party. Thanks to you we have it all. Right now there's a plane flying from England to the Canary Islands, to pick up General Francisco Franco. If things go as planned, by summer the military loyal to the uprising will have seized state power."

"What about the workers and the school children?"

"Don't worry, we've got them by the balls now and they're going to do what we say whether they like it or not. Hitler and Mussolini are going to send troops, infantry, mechanized artillery and also aviation. We're going to sweep away those assholes in the blink of an eye." Now he smiled, satisfied. "It's all been discussed, when you return to Germany, you'll have a position as a race car driver with the best team. Tonight you go back home, there's a plane waiting for you."

"Commander, I just need to do one more thing, I can convince the anarchists and unionists."

"Do what you think is right." He said it angrily as he turned to leave the room. "If you'd rather stay on the ground to see the storm coming, good luck."

Richard, powerless, unleashed his anger by punching the wall. He still thought something could be done, that the inevitable could be avoided. The cards had been dealt, the certainty of a catastrophic end that he refused to admit.

He had arranged to meet Tomás at his house, to go to Málaga for the wedding of one of his many cousins on his mother's side. The marriage was first the traditional church ceremony and then according to the Gypsy rite.

"Come on, man. I thought you weren't coming." He didn't scold him, he said it with concern.

"Sorry, I had some last minute setbacks."

"What happened to you?" He noticed the wound on his hand, it still had fresh blood on the flayed knuckles.

"It's nothing, it was silly."

"Let me take a look." He gently took his hand.

He washed the wound with a hot cloth, then disinfected it with alcohol and bandaged it.

While close relatives followed the liturgy, the rest had a few beers at the corner bar. Then in a large Andalusian-style courtyard, with pots hanging from the flower-filled walls with geraniums and carnations, the real celebration began. All of Tomás's relatives seemed to be artists. Those who didn't play guitar, sang or danced flamenco like true professionals. Richard also thought at that moment about the mix of blood that flowed through his friend's veins. That was surely where his artistic side came from, his poetic way of seeing life.

The newlyweds were very young, love made them oblivious to what was happening in the country. Tomás's cousin, the groom, Juan Pedro Hernández, worked with his father in peddling, they had a cart and a mule, they set up stalls at the flea markets within a twenty kilometer radius, selling the espadrilles with esparto soles that they made themselves. Juampe was eighteen and his wife María del Rosario had just turned sixteen, she was four months pregnant and already showing. She was a dark and beautiful girl, used to working hard at home taking care of her eight younger siblings. They looked happy. At a time when many people married for convenience or obligation - girls working as maids who got pregnant by young masters and were forced to marry much older bachelors - they were the exception. They had known each other since they were children and already played at simulating their wedding when they were eight and six years old respectively. In addition to being young and attractive, he had a trade and she knew very well what hard work was, taking care of her siblings, her sick father and mother, it was a full time job.

The guests got up to say a few words to the newlyweds, followed by songs, poetry and jokes by some comedians; but the funniest part of the night was seeing the German dancing the Sevillanas. The celebration lasted three days, people rested by sleeping for a while sitting on chairs or lying on the floor, but soon someone would warn that fresh fried rosquillas with chocolate or coffee, sweet wine fritters, borrachuelos, sponge cakes, tortas, churros and porras were ready. Sweets soaked in alcohol, anise, brandy, grape pomace brandy, wines and beers, even the grandmothers ended up drunk. When they couldn't take it anymore, in the early morning of the third day they decided to return to Almeria.

71

They staggered drunkenly through the streets of Malaga, looking for a taxi or bus to get back home, but had no idea where they were going. Dawn was breaking and they were climbing the steep slope of a cobbled street. He slowly lowered his head onto the German's shoulder, resting his cheek. Without stopping walking, he took his hand. When Richard turned around surprised and looked at him, Tomás kissed him on the mouth.

"What the fuck's the matter with you?" Richard shoved him, almost knocking him to the ground.

Tomás didn't say anything, he came up to him, put his hands around his neck and kissed him again. The two grappled in hand-to-hand combat. Opposing desires and feelings. The beauty of young passion between two lovers. The explosion of color on a Vincent Van Gogh canvas, the breaking of established norms in Pablo Picasso's cubic strokes, love in a verse, in a sonnet by Federico Garcia Lorca.

The flickering morning light brought sharp feelings to Richard's mind. He didn't quite remember or didn't want to remember exactly what happened last night. He didn't really know how to react. The feeling of guilt or perhaps shame. The judgment others might make of it all. He prefers to leave, without saying anything, to take some distance to see things in perspective. To reflect on the matter. He had never been attracted to any woman, to any one in particular, he had some female friends but nothing more than that.

Tomás, on the other hand, knew very well what he wanted. He had felt attracted to men all his life and had been in love with Richard since day one. When he saw him leave that morning without saying anything, he felt the irrational fear of never seeing him again. He didn't hear from him for several days, when he finally appeared, he didn't seem like the same person, he addressed Tomás in a distant way, as if they barely knew each other.

"Let's forget about the other day, as far as I'm concerned nothing happened. I'm not like you." His words sounded inert, devoid of feeling.

They spent the rest of the day together without talking about it again. They walked from village to village meeting with party members, leaders who relayed first-hand information about what was happening in the area, adding their own proposals. The dust from the road embedded in their shoes and trouser legs. Tomás liked doing it this way, the path is made by walking. Arriving by car in small towns and farming villages seemed wrong. That was for the landowners and their foremen hunting for day laborers. Getting out of a flashy Hispano-Suiza J12, with shoes clean as a whistle and offering coins to the best workers. Knowing it is they who refuse to distribute the wealth, plunging the population into poverty.

—Ninety-nine point nine percent of those of us born poor will die poor. Since I'm going to be poor all my life, I declare myself a writer, I'm a poet. I don't plan on collecting their harvest. — That was how Tomás saw it.

When they got back walking the moonlit roads at night, Richard stopped him by putting a hand on his shoulder, then without saying anything kissed him. The first unsure contact, with reluctance, then they let everything go and right there on the grass on the roadside they came together. This time it was more real, without the intoxicating effect clouding his judgment.

"I'm sorry!" Richard whispered, apologizing for his behavior. For the offensive words he had directed at him that very morning.

The first caresses were tender, almost childish, amid hugs and kisses. Tomás unbuttoned his white linen button-down Bagutta shirt. Leaving his chest and torso bare.

Chapter 16

Clandestine Loves

THE SPRING DAYS WERE very warm that year. Richard could spend hours without saying a word, observing the landscape while Tomás observed him. The sea water was icy, but the sun heated strongly and after a quick dip, they ran naked along the beach. Playing and frolicking carefree like teen lovers. They had to keep up appearances, no one could find out about them, about their love and sexual orientation. In 1936 people had many prejudices, especially in rural areas. His credibility as a union leader would be questioned. There were several young girls chasing after Tomás, so he decided to go out with one, nothing serious, just spending some afternoons together walking and talking around the city center, so everyone could see them. The oldest way of silencing some voices, of shutting their mouths. But he didn't want to deceive anyone, to use a nice girl that way, make her have false hopes only to dump her later. Now it was Richard who didn't understand that way of acting.

"What do other people's opinions matter?" He was tired of hiding and seeing him walk around with that girl.

"Are you serious?" His tone was gruff. "I fight for my people, I've been working for years to make things better, I can't toss it all away for my own interest."

"But it's more than that, these are our lives and I only have one."

"I don't expect you to understand. What would you know about sacrifice?" The tension was building.

"I'm not the young master who plays at saving day laborers, the boy who spends his time living life, drinking wine and writing poetry. I risk my life in every race and I've come very close to losing it. However much life I have left, ten months or ten years, I want to live them by your side."

That softened the poet's heart, leaving him speechless for once. But the next day he found him strolling again with the young Paquita. He crossed paths with them head-on, but didn't greet or acknowledge them. Then they met at the party meeting and afterwards went to the tavern. They seemed to have put some distance between them. Tomás couldn't stop looking at him, watching as the German flirted with a tramp. He bought her several drinks and after groping her in public, they went upstairs where there was a bedroom set up for that kind of thing.

They entered the hovel, a small room with a bed and next to it a washbasin and pitcher with water to rinse the genitals before proceeding with the act. He gave her some bills upfront.

"Most pay after, some even try to leave without paying." She was still young and beautiful, although the tiredness reflected in her face and eyes made her seem older.

She started to undress him but he pushed her away, then she proceeded to take off her dress. But the German interrupted her.

"How much do I have for this?" He referred to the money he had just handed her.

"You have a full hour."

He was sitting on the edge of the bed and she was standing, she had thrown the dress on the floor and looked at him in her underwear. Her skin was very white, as if she had never been out in the sun and her body and figure were slim and pretty. She had shapely legs and a pert, eye-catching but small behind. He took everything he had in his wallet and handed it to the woman.

"With this you have at least two hours, lie down on the bed and rest for a while." She agreed without questioning. Soon she was snoring like a bear, while Richard, fully dressed in shirt, pants and shoes, lay reclined on the bed smoking a cigarette calmly.

TOMÁS GARCÍA HERNÁNDEZ had spent all day pacing in circles with a half-smoked cigarette between his lips, he didn't usually smoke, he had a pipe at home that he sometimes used as a prop, as it gave him an intellectual, seasoned poet air. That morning he had bought a pack of Continental blondes, and had one left. He was nervous waiting for Beckenbauer to show up in town. His impeccable white shirt and pleated flannel pants contrasted with the worn soles of his shoes. He looked like a boy on his first date. When he finally saw him appear he ran up the street. The German waited for him with open arms, looked around for a second and pushed him forcefully, almost dragging him, until taking shelter on a corner, where he kissed him fiercely.

"I shouldn't even look at you, last night you fucked that whore." He was jealous and Richard knew it.

"I spent two hours lying in bed, smoking and staring at the ceiling, while the poor woman let her pussy rest for a while. She snored like a truck driver. I did it all to make you jealous."

They both looked at each other laughing, then went back to kissing. Paquita came out of nowhere and stared at them, hurried by flushed when she recognized them, then once far enough away she stopped and burst into tears. She felt stupid and thought that maybe Tomás had turned homosexual because of her. For not having been more direct, maybe she made it too difficult, too complicated and he finally got bored.

"You should talk to Paquita, what you're doing is not right." The other nodded.

And that same afternoon he went looking for her at her parents' house. She used to skip down the steps when he waited for her and now she went slowly, eyes downcast. Before he could say a word to her she burst into tears, the poor girl crying inconsolably.

"I'm sorry, it's my fault." She said between sobs.

"The fault of what?" Tomás adjusted his glasses by pressing the bridge with his index finger.

He couldn't understand what she was talking about. He gave her his handkerchief to dry her face and after a while she spilled everything. That she had seen him kissing the German and it was all her fault, but that if he wanted she could still spread her legs. Then he had no choice but to explain everything, telling her the story from the beginning. He said he had been that way since he was a little boy, that he was very sorry to have deceived her.

"You already know Paquita, no worker would listen to a faggot, and many would enjoy watching me hanged from an olive tree." The young woman's gaze was sweet and understanding.

Tomás would never have thought she would understand, but Paquita hugged him affectionately, as if they were siblings.

"I've always admired you and been very fond of you, this makes you more special, your secret is safe with me." Her tear reddened, irritated eyes cleared with her smile.

In her joy she gave him a kiss on the lips and she was left surprised. Then they went for a walk, strolling through the streets of Almeria and stopped at a stand to buy some ice cream. As they turned around, they came face to face with Richard. The German lowered his head, as if he didn't want to see them; but Paquita called out to him. The whole street was watching them and he froze, not knowing what to do, whether to approach the seemingly deranged young woman or run down the street. He pretended not to have heard her, but she shouted his name

77

even louder. He approached them sheepishly, making a gentlemanly greeting with his hat.

"Come here handsome, grab this arm." With linked arms. On one side walked Tomás and on the other the German.

Paquita spoke in a strange way, Richard thought she might be drunk. But when they reached the beach she finally told everything. She left them on a rocky area.

"Behave yourselves boys, I'm going to look for shells on the shore." And before leaving she winked at them emphatically, making them laugh.

Chapter 17

Nighttime Sabotage

SEEING THE DIRECTION events were taking, Richard decided to act on his own. At night and armed only with a knife, he went to the mine. He found the trucks parked there. At first, before the Germans arrived everything was done on the backs of donkeys, carrying the ore from the mine to the ships at the port. But now they had a French Somua truck, a one-ton Ford A and a ZIS-5 made in Russia. Several German trucks were scheduled to arrive for expanding the mine. Carefully trying not to make noise he cut all the engine wiring and water and fuel hoses, then tried to slash the tires, but it was more difficult than he had imagined, he had to use a rock to hit the base of the knife and manage to pierce the rubber. After putting all the vehicles out of service, he went up to the runway and entered the hangar.

"This is going to hurt me more than it hurts you." He said softly to the Junkers trimotor, before starting to cut wires and hoses.

An act of outright sabotage, which kept the mine from operating for a few days and best of all, they couldn't send the plane to help General Francisco Franco. At that moment, he didn't think about the consequences, he was full of anger, tired of putting up with everything and doing nothing. In a world gone mad, perhaps the only reasonable acts are those one does for others, without worrying about one's own benefit. He had been in Almeria for almost a year and felt like just another miner, a day laborer or peasant working those barren lands with his hands.

A beautiful but exhausting day of work for Baena. Watering and tending livestock, as well as party work, he was in charge of going to the print shop and distributing pamphlets and informational prints to party headquarters. Early in the morning before going to the print shop, he had to mow to feed the livestock, then in Almeria he had a carajillo at the bar. The coffee with brandy gave him energy for the rest of the morning, after eating he finished off with a couple shots of cognac. His two young companions helped load the truck and on the way to Malaga they stopped in every small village to hand out pamphlets, put up posters and give some brief revolutionary speeches, although the latter - speaking in public - wasn't his forte. Tomás and Richard were in charge of gathering people in the squares and speaking to them. Bear in mind that in those times most people couldn't read, it was essential for someone to explain to them the state of the country. Then in the afternoon he continued with his chores: milking the sheep, watering and digging in the garden and finally when he was done, hoe over his shoulder, he headed home along the path near the coast, through the hills bordering the cliffs. He sat on a rock looking out to sea from above, took out a pack of rolling papers and a pouch of tobacco, skillfully rolling himself a cigarette. Black tobacco without a filter, cut for men. A direct stab to the lungs. He looked at the sky and sea, the coastline and a white sailboat cruising the horizon into infinity. Seeing such beauty made him want to shit. At the edge of the cliff among the bushes he dropped his pants and proceeded while enjoying the wondrous views. While he was in the middle of it, he saw people on the beach, Paquita walking barefoot along the shore and then scrutinizing the area more thoroughly he felt a punch in the gut when he made out Tomás hugging the German. He pulled up his pants without wiping his ass and crouched among the bushes, clenching his sphincter for fear of being discovered. Things got worse when they started kissing. He stayed there, not missing a single detail.

Chapter 18

Pure Gold

THE COMMOTION OUTSIDE woke them as they lay embraced in bed, they looked at each other surprised trying to figure out what was going on in the street, voices and shouts could be heard through the window of the double room with two beds at La Marismeña boardinghouse.

"We have to go out and see what's happening." Richard hurried to get dressed.

"Don't forget to mess up the other bed." Tomás pointed out while looking for his socks on the floor.

Richard pulled back the sheets and jumped on with his shoes still on.

"Done, let's go now."

People were upset, restlessly running back and forth with newspapers in hand. They had to stop a boy to explain what had happened. Lieutenant of the Assault Guard José Castillo had been murdered by the far-right and in revenge that same night the guards went looking for Calvo Sotelo at his home, took him by force and in the morning he was found dead.

Nerves were on edge, anarchists slept in newspaper offices and party headquarters had people sprawled on the floor everywhere, waiting for bad news at any moment, notice of the coup d'etat, the outbreak of civil war. And so it happened, the murders were the fuse that lit the powder keg. Until now General Franco refused to move, he was waiting for something that would really justify armed action and this was perfect timing. He immediately took command of the Spanish Legion and the African army. They were professional soldiers with extensive combat experience from the war in Africa. The first problem they encountered was moving the troops from Africa to the mainland, he managed to cross the first ship with soldiers, but the sailors loyal to the Republic mutinied against their commanders, taking control of most of the ships, leaving Franco and his troops isolated. The general contacted Commander Uli Lindemann by phone, after quelling the mining revolt in Asturias the Germans were in his debt, plus if they wanted to continue taking away the tungsten the only option left to them was to support the rebels. The commander requested the German air force send transport aircraft so the troops could cross over. The mine director contacted Mussolini himself and asked for a dozen Savoia Marchetti SM 81s to join the German Junkers Ju 52s in Tetouan. He ordered Christoph Schneider to head there with the mining company's plane.

There was an important town meeting held in Almeria's main square, the different leaders of the parties loyal to the Republic debated how to proceed. There were continuous interruptions from people who disagreed and shouted insults. Some wanted to stay calm, wait and see how things evolved, they weren't aware of the storm headed their way. On the other hand, Pepe Baena's group proposed distributing weapons among the population, and jailing the Falangists. Even better, trying them publicly and getting rid of them. Baena seemed deranged, in the heat of his speech he incited people to go up to the Rodalquilar mine and throw out the Germans. If the population followed him it would turn into a bloodbath, a massacre, and Beckenbauer knew it.

"Comrades, brothers and sisters, we must stay calm. With your permission I will go up to the mine to negotiate an agreement. If we yield tungsten exploitation we can get the Nazis to withdraw their support for the fascists." Richard thought there was still room for dialogue with the mine director.

"Shut up German, you don't know what you're talking about." Baena interrupted him, shoving him out of the square center.

From insults they moved on to blows, they started fist fighting. Richard landed several direct hits to the jaw that left Baena almost unconscious, he remained on his feet but his head was spinning and he didn't know where he was. The others watched in a circle around them as if it were a boxing match. He rubbed his face for a moment with his hands and wiped the blood from them onto the leg of his corduroy pants. Then instead of giving up and letting Beckenbauer speak, he took a knife from his pocket.

"Comrade, I'm not talking about surrendering, what I want is for Germany to reconsider its stance. Guaranteeing mining resources in exchange for a non-intervention policy."

"You're not my comrade. You're not even Spanish."

He lunged at his side, slashing his linen shirt, missing his flesh by mere millimeters. Before he could make another thrust, hitting him in the face again managed to disarm him. Then he spoke again to everyone:

"I'm one of you, I'll stay and fight to the end, this is my country now. But with all the sorrow in my heart, before attacking, we must try to talk. It's just tungsten, it's not worth any of our lives."

"It's not just tungsten." Baena interrupted again, wiping his face with his shirtsleeve to clean off the blood. "They are our resources, the riches of our country. They're taking the gold to Germany and leaving us with rubble."

"The gold?" Richard asked, confused.

That was when he found out that the Rodalquilar mines were not tungsten, they were extracting pure gold to take to Germany.

The gold found in the Rodalquilar mines is of volcanic origin. Extraction had been attempted for decades, but lack of technology made it unfeasible. The Nazis had advanced machinery to accomplish it. Gold was discovered in 1915 at the María Josefa mine. The fledgling mining companies were small cooperatives formed by local miners, who failed in their attempt. The first German company to work in Rodalquilar was Krupp Grusonwerk in the 1930s. The complex known as the Dorr Plant had agitator tanks to carry out the cyanidation process, it was chaired by the Marquis of Arriluce de Ybarra, although the majority of shares were in British hands. The Dorr Plant produced a thousand kilos of gold in a very short time, production was halted at the start of the Civil War. Richard Beckenbauer had been deceived all this time, of course he wasn't an engineer and that's probably why they chose him. Now the pieces fit together in his head, Spanish gold was filling the coffers of the German state. His brother must have been aware of everything and for some reason became a hindrance.

Chapter 19

Conviction without Trial

THE MINING BASE WAS chaos, more soldiers had arrived and everyone was running around in turmoil. The directors, president and engineers were getting ready to return to Berlin, while the complex was left in the hands of Commander Uli Lindemann and his men. Two soldiers were waiting for him at the entrance, they handcuffed him and forcibly took him before the commander.

"Son of a bitch!" Was what he said as soon as he saw him.

When he got close he punched him in the solar plexus, leaving him breathless. Richard was trying in vain to explain what was happening, but the commander wasn't listening, all he did was pace back and forth nervously in the room, pounding one fist into the other while cursing, spewing all kinds of foul language forming sentences of schizophrenic German grammar. He suspects, if not is certain, that he was the one who sabotaged the mine vehicles. Without trucks they couldn't continue extracting gold, but what infuriated him even more was looking like an idiot before the Führer. He had promised to send the Junkers to help transport troops from one continent to another. It had been sabotaged in such a way that two mechanics had been working on it for over twenty-four hours and couldn't repair it. Handcuffed with his hands behind his back and a Nazi holding each arm, they kept him on his feet before the commander. He came over and punched him again, this time more angrily.

"Take this traitor away from my sight!" He wiped his hands on the handkerchief he had taken from his pocket.

The sky suddenly turned black and it started pouring, fat drops fell on the Opel Olympia's windows stained with yellowish clay. Michael Horten called the teacher who was at school and told her they had detained Richard. Diane Klum drove the muddy roads to the mine, which in an instant turned into fast flowing rivers of clay. She skidded into the mining compound with the car and left it right at the door of the central building, where the director's office was located. In the hallway Michael Horten was waiting for her.

"What the hell happened?" She was nervous and irritated.

"The commander thinks Beckenbauer was the one who wrecked the trucks."

"I thought this was a civilian project, why have the military taken over the plant?" Diane was unaware of what was happening in the country.

Michael briefly explained the situation, he knew a bit more because Richard had told him. In Almeria they were preparing to take control of the mine. At the same time, the Civil War had begun in Spain, and apparently, despite non-intervention policies the Germans and Italians had decided to side with the rebels.

"I demand right now that you release Richard and let him defend himself." She barged into the director's office yelling. The little man was busy rummaging through reports in the filing cabinet.

She managed to get one last meeting in the conference room. There were the four of them, Commander Lindemann, pacing nervously around the room, the ever more absent-minded president of the mine. Engineer Michael Horten and her, after a bit they brought in the handcuffed Richard.

"Take it easy, take it easy, no need to shove, I can walk by myself." He reprimanded them for the shove they had just given him upon entering.

"This is ridiculous!" Diane protested. "Who do you think you are? We are Germans, the war is between Spaniards. Haven't you heard?"

"This traitor sabotaged us." The commander barked angrily.

Michael Horten immediately intervened, coming to his defense.

"That's impossible, the night the trucks were smashed we were both at the village bar. I have witnesses who can corroborate it." He was very nervous, lying wasn't his forte, but he blurted it out boldly.

"Commander Uli, I think you are overstepping, anyone could have gotten into the mine at night, the village is full of anarchists. Accusing Richard and detaining him is petty."

For a few seconds everyone was silent, the commander now paced slowly, weighing the possibility that he had been mistaken. Then unrelentingly bent on achieving peace in the area, Beckenbauer continued trying to engage in dialogue.

"There is no guarantee that this General Franco can overthrow the Republic. Taking sides is playing with fire. The most sensible thing would be to sign that non-intervention treaty with the other nations. That way whatever happens we could maintain the concession."

"I'm tired of listening to you, don't give me that story now." Lindemann had the folder with all the reports Richard had been submitting to him throughout the year. He read one of them aloud. "The anarchists will never allow excavations to expand, destroying the environment, and they will never work for the Nazis, helping them extract ore to manufacture armaments for Hitler. They are poor people, but they aren't idiots, they won't sell their souls to the devil."

"I wrote that a long time ago." He confessed.

"Exactly, when you were on our side, before going over to the enemy." Those were the only words the director uttered throughout the entire meeting.

Chapter 20

The Beginning of the End

PEPE BAENA WAS GIVING instructions at party headquarters, he had the support of the majority. He was already fed up with so much nonsense, he had decided to enter the mine at night, first seize the explosives and after gunning down the Nazi soldiers take control of the mining base. That action would strengthen the Republic, with control of the Rodalquilar mines they could continue extracting gold during the war, to pay for the armaments arriving from Russia and Mexico. It was a very dangerous operation, they were going to confront professional well-armed soldiers. They only had some hunting shotguns and three stolen rifles from the civil guard barracks. That's why Baena was preparing the assault meticulously, they would wait for the right time attacking at dawn. Tomás García was in southern Malaga, organizing the militiamen to confront the Italian and African troops already arriving on the mainland. They designed an extensive defensive line, trenches and bunkers, but weapons were scarce, so far no country had offered assistance. It was truly ironic and surrealistic, the European dictators were helping each other: Adolf Hitler from Germany, Benito Mussolini in Italy, Antonio de Oliveira Salazar in Portugal and even Joseph Stalin helped the Nazi pilots by training them at a secret base. Many of the Russian instructors who taught the Germans to fly were later sent to Spain to fight them in the air.

An encrypted message arrived for the commander. The soldier in charge of communications put it into the Enigma machine and handed it to him. In an instant he turned red with fury, shredded the paper and headed to the room where Richard was being held.

"Traitorous dog!" He shouted, spitting at the same time.

Richard was exhausted from the long hours he had been gagged to the chair. He didn't understand that sudden outburst of anger. Commander Lindemann took his 9mm Luger P08 semi-automatic with eight cartridges in the magazine from its leather holster, cocked it and held it to his temple. There was silence and Beckenbauer closed his eyes thinking this was the end. Curiously he didn't think of himself, he remembered Tomás's full lips, his smile, his intelligent gaze behind his intellectual glasses, his speeches and poetry. Then he felt intense pain in his cheek and ringing in his ear from the blow.

"I won't waste bullets on you, I'll hand you over to the authorities for you to be tried in Germany, that will be much more painful, you'll spend your last days in prison tortured by the SS and when they've knocked out your last tooth they'll hang you."

"You're crazy, you've lost your mind..."

"Crazy? It seems an Italian fighter patrolling near the Deutschland battleship was shot down by a Bücker. Not only are you a spy but a traitor to the fatherland. You informed those communists where our ships are hiding." Now he was taking off his belt.

He began beating him with the leather strap, his white shirt turned red. When he tired of lashing out blows he spoke out of breath:

"Rudolf, your little brother, also switched sides. I had to inform the Gestapo, they took care of it. They specialize in exterminating rat plagues."

THE SPRING OF 1937 was one of the rainiest. The Italians began the attack on the Guadalajara front, but the storm delayed their advance, giving the Republican army time to reorganize with reinforcements from Madrid. The Nationalist planes couldn't take off, the airfields turned into mud pits by the rain ceased to be operational, while the Republican air force had paved runways and the Russian planes at the Barajas, Guadalajara and Alcala de Henares bases destroyed numerous trucks stuck in the mud. It was one of the most prominent triumphs of the Republican air force.

Chapter 21

The Escape

THE COMMANDER SPOKE with the mine director, then they sent communications to Berlin and from the operations center informed the German fleet anchored at the port of Ibiza. The warships immediately set in motion, heading toward the coast of Almeria. The Lufthansa pilot Christoph Schneider who now worked for the mine, received orders to use the Junkers Ju 52 to bomb the city. They wanted to prepare incendiary bombs by filling barrels with gasoline and adding dynamite. Pilot Christoph tried to buy as much time as possible, delaying the transition from passenger plane to bomber. Two soldiers were patrolling and monitoring everything in the hangar.

"Stop! Where do you think you're going?" An armed guard blocked his path.

"What do you think?" He lowered his head looking at his feet and when the soldier did the same, he wiggled his toes in the open-toed espadrilles. "I need my uniform, boots and helmet."

He needed to find Diane or Michael, they had to stop the Nazis. He found them in the common dining room, Diane was smoking nervously thinking about what they could do. If Commander Lindemann had given orders to the German navy, surely the bombing would take place early in the morning. They had to warn the people to evacuate the city. If they went down there, even counting on not being shot and being allowed to speak, no one would believe them. They needed to free Richard, he could convince them. They had to rescue him and take him to the city, so he could inform Tomás and his family, they would sound the alarm.

"We have to think of something." Diane brought her hand to her forehead. "And fast."

"Maybe I can get him out, if you get the car ready we can take him down to Almeria." Horten hadn't been outside all day.

"Impossible, the roads are impassable, the rain has turned them into rivers of mud." She shook her head. "I can barely make it up, plus they've reinforced surveillance at the entrance checkpoint."

A German soldier stood guard in front of the door. Still, without moving a muscle, he looked like a statue. Michael Horten approached him with dinner on a metal tray, sausages and red beans.

"Good evening. Dinner for the traitor. Are you sure you haven't had dinner?" The engineer got very nervous every time he had to lie and overacted.

"I haven't been informed of anything." He said seriously breaking his rigid stance.

"Well I was ordered to bring dinner."

"One second, I'll check."

The tray almost fell to the floor because of his nerves, he had no idea what to do, so without thinking he smashed it on the soldier's head. He had to hit him three more times to knock him out. Then he dragged him inside the room, while Diane and Christoph came running down the hall to help. Michael untied Richard as quickly as he could.

"My God what have they done to you!" The doctor exclaimed when she saw his face stained with dried blood.

She helped him take off his shirt and then put on the soldier's shirt with the military jacket over it. The teacher cleaned his face with a handkerchief, touching him up with the tip wet with saliva.

"You'd better put on the cap too."

Horten suggested taking one of the trucks, since they were taller and their wheels were designed to drive on dirt and mud.

"But how are we going to get through the checkpoint?"

"Is the Junkers still operational?" Richard looked at Christoph and he nodded.

"It's ready in the hangar."

"We have to hurry, time plays in our favor."

It was barely raining now, black clouds with a lot of lightning covered the sky. A flash of lightning lit up the bedroom and Commander Uli Lindemann woke up with a start, as if he had dreamed what was happening. He was lying on the cot, dressed in shirt, pants and boots. He sat up on the edge, put on his suspenders and went out without his jacket. When he got to the door he was surprised to find the guard wasn't there. He saw beans on the floor. Before going in he took out his gun from the holster, carefully opened the door and made sure there was no one else in the room. When he saw the prisoner tied to the chair he put away the weapon and relaxed for a moment. He looked at the floor and when he saw he was wearing military pants and boots, he grabbed him by the hair lifting his head to be able to see his face, then he realized it was a hoax. He rushed out to sound the alarm, but the Junkers was already on the runway. The commander ran uphill toward the airfield. The three engines roared at full power.

"We're not going to make it, the runway is too soft." Christoph told Richard who was next to him in the copilot seat.

The mud slowed the plane's wheels reducing its speed. Visibility was almost nil, the darkness of night and rain on the windshield prevented seeing the end of the runway.

"There's no turning back now. Full throttle and may God's will be done." Diane was behind them, while engineer Michael Horten in the rear put on a parachute as if it would save his life.

The commander reached the top of the hill where the runway ended. The tri-motor's propellers spun toward him. He stood firm, in shooting stance and unloaded the eight rounds from his 9mm Luger semiautomatic through the pilot's door. At the last second he threw himself flat on the ground, sinking into the mud, the plane took off barely missing him by inches.

"We made it!" Diane shouted euphorically.

Horten thanked God. The plane banked strangely and began losing altitude. Richard looked to his left and saw two projectiles had hit the pilot. One in the chest and another in the neck that killed him almost instantly. He hurriedly took the controls trying to stabilize the aircraft. Diane Klum examined Christoph checking his pulse, but there was nothing to be done, he was dead.

"You have to get him out of there, I need you as co-pilot, I can't land this crate alone." Beckenbauer had managed to level it off, but touching down was another story.

He was able to orient himself thanks to the city lights. Having flown the coast so many times and walked the area was very helpful. He knew of a large beach very near Almeria, it was the ideal place to land. Diane had to help him with the Junkers' heavy controls. If he managed to put the plane down on the beach, the headwind would help him land in less space, to be able to brake before crashing into the rocks. He flew high among the clouds and couldn't see anything, as they descended he thought they would crash against the cliff peaks, but they got lucky, at low elevation everything seemed clear, the city lights reflected on the water, showing the sandy area as if it were a runway.

"When I tell you, pull back on the controls as hard as you can." She nodded.

When the landing gear was about to touch ground he gave the order and pulling with all her might they managed to lift the nose, the plane bounced several times. Michael in the rear was screaming in terror.

"Dear God I don't want to die." He sobbed.

The sturdy landing gear withstood the punishment, the fine sand on the beach helped brake. Now Richard's concerns were others, to get to the city as soon as possible and warn Tomás, he had to alert the people before the bombing began.

"It's best if you two stay here, I'll try to send someone to help camouflage the plane." He ran off toward the port of Almeria.

He arrived at El Cortijo tavern soaked to the bone, the bartender served him a drink to warm up.

"I need to talk to Tomás García." The bartender was one of the party's political secretaries and was well informed.

"It's not a good time." With his eyes he signaled the people sitting at a table in the back. "Not everyone's oregano."

Richard didn't understand Spanish jokes and sayings, but deduced not everyone supported the Republic, that there were fascists among the people. Some acted on their own and others were spies sent by the Francoists, police and civil guards on secret missions. Infiltrating enemy territory and causing as much damage as possible. At night you had to be careful, snipers could shoot from any terrace.

"It's a matter of life and death." Sincerity was his best play.

"Stop by and see Basi, you know where she lives and walk under the balconies, don't get too wet."

He headed to Tomás's house, heeding the warning, he walked fast and tried not to be an open target. To run across streets, not stop at corners or cut across lit doors and windows. The house lights were off, he knocked on the door with his hand, no one answered. He waited a couple minutes and insisted once more. Now he heard footsteps down the hall, the latch sounded and Mrs. Basilisa opened up.

"Come in, come in, don't stand there!"

"I need to talk to Tomás, the Germans are going to bomb tomorrow, everyone must be warned."

"Tomás is at the party, go warn him, I'll alert the others."

He ran again in the rain, crossing streets until he reached the anarchist headquarters. A man stood guard at the door.

"I need to talk to Tomás."

"What Tomás?" As if he didn't know what he was talking about, as if he didn't know him.

"It's urgent damn it, cut the bullshit."

He opened the door without saying anything else. Inside they were loudly debating something. Seeing him enter they all fell silent. Tomás called Pepe Baena over to replace him.

"What are you doing here?" Although he would have liked to kiss and hug him, Tomás kept his distance.

He told him he needed to speak with him privately for a moment. They went into the small room where his mother had the virgin illuminated with candles. Then upon closing the door he gave him an intense kiss. Then he began telling him everything, he didn't really know how to do it, or how he would take it, but so many secrets were burning him up inside. He couldn't take it anymore, he had to get it out. He told him he had come to Spain to do espionage work for the mining company. Try to convince the miners to keep working and get the unionists to yield the exploitation to the Germans. That he had sent reports on all of them and thanks to him they knew in detail the entire party structure. At that point they started arguing, Tomás couldn't believe what he was hearing. Richard apologized and said he was very sorry, that it was all before really getting to know him, before falling in love. Now he no longer trusted him, he felt betrayed, deceived. He had given him everything, what he had and who he was, while Beckenbauer sold them out to the enemy.

"Out of my sight!" Tomás yelled unable to hold back the tears. "Get out and don't come back!"

He dried himself with his hands and ran out. Richard didn't have time to warn him, to tell him what was about to happen. He felt like a con man, a complete fraud. Despite the terrible pain in his chest, he had to move forward, go out there and warn everyone. Upon crossing the door he felt someone's presence right next to him, but before he could even look Pepe Baena hit him over the head with the butt of his shotgun. When he regained consciousness he was dizzy and in pain, he didn't remember where he was or what he was doing there. It took him several minutes to realize what was happening. Pepe Baena was aware of the reports he sent to the Germans and now they had him gagged accused of being a snitch. What was happening was nothing new, it was part of his life, he never belonged anywhere, everywhere they accused him of being a foreigner or traitor. Of course he never cared what people thought, the only thing that mattered was what Tomás might think. That tormented him.

"You're not laughing so much now faggot. I thought you had come to fuck the Spanish girls, like the rest of your countrymen, but I was wrong. Turns out the German came out a faggot."

Beckenbauer didn't understand how he had found out. He didn't really care all that much either, least of all at that moment. He only wished to disappear, to leave this world.

Chapter 22

The Bombing of Almeria

THEY HAD RICHARD GAGGED while they discussed when to execute him. For Baena he was just another Nazi, even worse; in his view he was a spy, an informant who had sold them out for pennies like Judas.

"Do what you have to do, but do it already." He wanted to die.

"You shut up faggot." Pepe yelled at him. "I make the decisions here."

And to think that when he was bedridden in the hospital he thought he couldn't feel more pain. Now his body was healthy, it was his heart that was shattered and the suffering much more intense. An unbearable stab in the chest that wouldn't let him breathe. He felt dizzy when he remembered Tomás, his neatly trimmed, jet black beard like his hair and his sensitive, tender and intelligent eyes behind his round tortoise shell glasses. And remembering his fleshy lips and warm kisses, tears welled up in his eyes.

"I'm despicable, just kill me already." He cried in pain over what he had done.

Tomás García had taken him in like a brother and he had betrayed him. For his own interest, first tempted by Commander Lindemann's offer, to return to Berlin with a spot on one of the top racing teams and later deceiving himself with Diane Klum's ideas, the stupid utopia of happy miners and a school full of children. Not to mention that while robbing them of their wealth by taking away the gold, they were killing them by polluting the land and poisoning the air.

"Get him on his feet." Baena ordered the two boys who usually accompanied him. "Out to the yard, we're going to shoot him."

Richard didn't resist, he remained absentminded as they dragged him across the floor. The rain had stopped, the cement floor was still puddled. The decision had been made, it was best to get rid of the German, they planned on storming the mining base and couldn't leave him loose to alert his compatriots.

"Put him there against the wall."

They left him in front, his wrists tied behind his back with a sisal rope. Pepe pointed his pistol at his head, ready to shoot.

"Cover his face damn it, he's staring at me." He couldn't shoot looking into his eyes.

One of the boys took a burlap sack and put it over his head. Now all three of them aimed at him, Pepe with the pistol and the other two with shotguns.

"Stop! Freeze you jackasses." He lowered the pistol angrily and slapped the back of the neck of the one next to him. "Not with the shotguns, you'll turn him into chopped meat and then who's going to clean up the mess."

Pepe Baena tried again on his own. Two meters away he aimed at the German's head, but his hand shook, through a hole in the sack he could see the greenish-blue color of his eyes.

"Fuck." He lowered the weapon. "Take the sack off, we're not like the fascists."

The two boys were relieved, they all knew Richard, they had shared bread and wine, dusty roads, union work and festival nights. He had been with them for over a year, he was there in the good times and the bad. Of course if he had done what they said, it was unforgivable.

"Just kill me already!" He shouted at them.

"Don't give me orders, damn German. Crazy bastard."

Finally Baena decided to hold him until the next day, once they had taken the mining base. After that he would have no one left to inform, they would set him free and let him fend for himself.

ON MAY 31 PEPE BAENA got up early as he did every morning, he started cutting alfalfa to feed the animals. When he looked out to sea, he saw a white cloud over the water, from the fog bank five ships of the German fleet appeared. The Admiral Scheer battleship emerged from the fog bank along with four destroyers: Leopard, Albatros, Lluchs and Seeadler. They approached through Mesa Roldán to Cabo de Gata and positioned themselves about twelve kilometers from the coast of Níjar. Baena ran to sound the alarm, but before his eyes, around seven thirty detonations began to be heard. The muzzle flashes exiting the cannon mouths could be seen clearly. When the shells began to rain down, Pepe and his whole family took shelter in a cave they had dug under a fig tree. It was indiscriminate bombing of the population of Almeria.

Commander Uli Lindemann had requested a punitive action from the German high command against the people of Almeria in retaliation for what happened at the mine. That attack was not considered until Republican planes, Tupolev SB-2 "Katyusha", that had left the Los Alcázares base in Murcia, bombed the Deutschland, a German battleship anchored at the port of Ibiza. It was then that Adolf Hitler approved the bombing of Almeria. The battleship spotted by Richard and Tomás was in Spanish waters, it had also violated the restriction not to approach within ten miles of the coast. It had broken all international non-intervention regulations. When Adolf Hitler was informed that the destroyer had been located by Republican aviation and subsequently attacked, he flew into a rage. It took the German foreign minister six hours to calm him down. Despite the great damage, the battleship was not sunk and returned to the German shipyards for repairs. Finally the Führer accepted the request made by Commander Uli Lindemann. Revenge came that morning, four German destroyers and the Admiral Scheer battleship positioned themselves near the coast and opened fire. They caused over thirty deaths and at no time tried to hide or camouflage their nationality. It was not a mission in support of the rebel troops, it was a military action coordinated by the German high command, openly attacking the Republic, but no one cared, British and French politicians looked the other way. For over an hour they indiscriminately bombarded the civilian population with two hundred and seventy-five cannon blasts. They hit the headquarters of the International Red Cross, they also damaged historic buildings like the Almeria Cathedral and the Church of San Sebastián, the market, the train station, the art school and city hall.

The Republican government, the council of ministers met to assess the response, they could send planes to the Mediterranean and sink the German ships, but that would lead to world war. Orders arrived from the Soviet Union not to intervene, the Russians didn't want to attack the Germans, they also lacked support from France and Great Britain. Finally President Manuel Azaña had to reject military action, fearing to cause even more civilian casualties. The Deutschland incident could somehow justify a German offensive, triggering World War II, but Hitler's armies were not yet ready. So the attack was forgotten.

In the party committee they had considered the possibility of a bombing and architect Guillermo Langle was commissioned to design underground shelters so the people of Almeria could take refuge. A complex of over four kilometers of tunnels was built that could accommodate ninety percent of the population, some forty thousand people.

If there were not two sides there would be no war. Guilty or not, someone threw the first stone, but the others didn't just stand there. And it is that mixture of compassion and mistrust that he felt when looking into the face of a survivor, a refugee. Only he knows what he was capable of and what he actually did. Tomás García mulled it over. He himself was part of both sides. Perhaps the only innocents in a war were children, because even women and the elderly may have contributed to it. Stockpiling every gram of gunpowder. Conspiracies, grudges, jealousy, snitching on some and hiding others for personal gain.

Richard lay curled up on the floor in the fetal position, locked in a room in the warehouse used as party headquarters. Something whistled overhead and instantly the blast and flash. Fire and destruction. The din woke him, he then knew the bombing had begun. He positioned himself in a corner, against the thick load-bearing walls. The explosions made the ground shake like an earthquake. The piercing sound of a projectile abruptly ended in an explosion that knocked down the thick adobe wall. His ears were ringing, he couldn't see anything and could barely breathe from the cloud of smoke and dust. He walked over the rubble, stumbling dazed among the ruins. He was covered head to toe in a gray layer, a red streak of blood ran down his forehead, breaking up the black and gray tones. He wanted to help, find Tomás, but shells were falling everywhere. People ran through the streets screaming, there were people trapped under the rubble. A woman walked down the street with a baby in her arms and a small child holding her hand, a second later she had disappeared under the debris. Richard started digging, removing the rubble with his hands, after a bit he uncovered the three lifeless bodies. Terror overcame him paralyzing him, he feared Tomás might suffer the same fate. He ran down the street toward his parents' house. He found Mr. Elías and his wife Basilisa, helping people enter the anti-aircraft tunnels. The subway entrance had collapsed, clogged by the stampede. Tomás's father and mother were trying to get people to enter calmly. Projectiles rained from the sky, one struck the nearby building which collapsed like a house of cards. In the cloud of dust Richard found the woman covered in dirt and disoriented, Elías had disappeared under the rubble and the tunnel entrance was plugged by several meters of dirt, concrete and bricks. Beckenbauer thought quickly, he looked around, there was barely any visibility, the dust cloud formed a fog wall, but he saw the party's Renault Vivasix. He helped Tomás's mother into the passenger seat, she was bleeding from a shrapnel wound on her arm. He slammed the gas without seeing where he was going. Leaving the cloud behind the clear blue sky appeared. He drove through the streets of Almeria at full speed, dodging craters and collapsed buildings from the bombs. He took the road toward Malaga, when he arrived in the city they were amazed at the number of people, refugees in the streets. The cathedral had become an improvised shelter.

"It's best if you stay here. I'm going back for Tomás."

At the cathedral door, they found a group of older women in black dresses and headscarves, in charge of several children. Basi recognized some of them, they were the mothers and wives of the Almeria anarchists, including Pepe Baena's mother.

"I'm so sorry." Said the woman who still wore mourning clothes for the death of Baena's brother. She embraced Mrs. Basilisa, giving her condolences. "Little Tomás is dead, I saw it with my own eyes, a bomb got him at the Almeria market."

Upon hearing that Richard felt his heart stop beating, his knees trembled and he had to sit for a moment on the cathedral entrance steps.

Chapter 23

Raid on the Mine

THE NIGHT BEFORE THE bombing of Almeria, the militia group led by Pepe Baena prepared in Almeria, moderately uniformed, with work overalls to which each added emblems of the CNT or FAI, some rifles had arrived and they also distributed cloth bags to transport ammunition. They rode in two Russian-made ZIS-5 open bed trucks. Obviously they couldn't approach through Rodalquilar and go directly up to the mine; they waited until nightfall, then departed on the national road toward Cartagena. They crossed Retamar, El Viso, San Isidro de Níjar, Campohermoso and in Venta del pobre took a road toward Rodalquilar. The last kilometers were done with the truck lights off, they went down the mountainsides and began a long night hike. Baena led the way.

"You, damn your dead." He raised a clenched fist to one of the militia member's face, who walked smoking calmly as if on an excursion. "Put that out now or I'll make you swallow it."

They advanced single file on the rocky mountainside. The terrain of sandstone and calcite crumbled under their feet. Pepe ordered them to form a long human chain, walking all in a line holding hands. This way they avoided plunging to the bottom of the gorge. The last five hundred meters were done in absolute silence, communicating only with hand signals. About two hundred meters away they gathered and lay on the ground waiting for several hours, until there was no movement seen or heard. With some clippers Baena cut the barbed wire and they headed toward the warehouse where the explosives were stored. The group included several mine workers who knew the terrain perfectly. They advanced building by building, placing explosives in the main ones, then the different groups readied themselves to detonate all the charges at the same time. Pepe Baena and his men waited at the main gate. As explosions occurred everywhere they pounced on the soldiers guarding, disarming them. Commander Uli Lindemann came out pistol in hand, thinking it wasn't that serious. As soon as he peered out several errant shots whistled over his head. He went back inside the building and fired out the window until he ran out of bullets. He ordered his soldiers to defend the central offices as he ran to the rear. Escaping through a small window in a room, he went into the mountainous area enveloped in the dark veil of night. The besieged soldiers didn't last long, as soon as they ran out of ammo they surrendered. There were several wounded, but no casualties. Among the prisoners was the mine director, they arrested him in his office burning confidential documents.

From that moment on and throughout the conflict the mine was in Republican hands, work continued on gold extraction - more necessary than ever - to be used in purchasing weapons. Due to the complicated circumstances, the lack of skilled miners and tools, a scarce production was obtained. The strong, young workers left for the Málaga front, led by Baena.

Commander Uli Lindemann bled from his left arm, the bullet had hit his shoulder. It wasn't a serious wound, but he had the back of his white shirt stained with blood. He walked through the hills at night heading west until he came upon the road. He continued along the ditch when a truck's lights blinded him. The vehicle stopped next to him and the driver got out to ask what had happened to him. The commander barely understood Spanish, he remained quiet without saying anything, standing in front of the truck's headlights under which the bloodstain shone. The man approached confidently seeing him injured and unarmed. When he was close enough the commander grabbed him by surprise, lunging at his neck. He tried to resist for a few seconds until he was left breathless. Lindemann wrapped his right arm around his neck in a death grip, squeezing with all his might. His feet began moving with the final convulsions and then he died. He took the greenish suede jacket, emptied the inside pocket contents, a worn wallet containing documentation and some money. He dragged him off the road, leaving him tossed behind the rock roses. Then he put on the jacket which was a bit short sleeved and got in the truck as if nothing had happened. He drove to the Nationalist zone in Seville. He entered a churro shop and asked for some phone tokens.

"Telefonieren?" He left a bill on the bar. "Danke."

He went into the small wooden phone booth at the back of the premises. He put the token in the black Bakelite telephone and angrily bellowed in German. Shortly after a black Mercedes Benz picked him up at the door and took him to the German embassy. There they bandaged his shoulder wound without asking questions, he requested new clothes and the ambassador gave him one of his suits. The commander looked at the teak wood floors, Persian rugs, chandeliers, exquisite works of art, sculptures, canvases by famous painters, valuable gold and silver objects. The commander who had spent the last few years living in the small compartment of the dusty mining base, looked with disdain at the glossy, fancied up, ostentatious ambassador. Comfortable bourgeois politicians, for them the word work means going to a banquet, a dinner and then chatting seated on a sofa with a glass of French cognac in one hand and a Montecristo cigar in the other about the Spanish war.

Commander Uli Lindemann directed the revenge operation from the bridge of the Admiral Scheer battleship. By seven in the morning they were already off the coast of Almeria. The fleet made up of the destroyer and battleships: Leopard, Albatros, Lluchs and Seeadler. The commander ordered the artillery to open fire. From the bridge with a cup of coffee in hand, he watched through binoculars as the shells fell on the population. He enjoyed watching the spectacle as if it were a fireworks display.

Chapter 24

The Road of Death

UNDER THE DEAFENING storm of bombs, people resisted as best they could. The ground shook under their feet, the death-filled air was dense, dark and unbreathable. Tomás García Hernández searched for his parents among the rubble. His body covered in dirt, smoke and dust, his clothes torn to shreds and bleeding cuts on his face and hands. He had miraculously survived, crawling under the debris. When he reached the area where his parents were he saw the destruction was greater. The collapsed buildings fell on the people trying to enter the underground shelters. He saw shoes on the ground and lifeless bodies of neighbors, comrades and friends revealed among the piles of dirt and ash. He approached and looked at the crushed face of a young woman. He recognized the dress, the shape of her body, the curly hair and the silver chain with a Christ that he himself had given Paquita. He felt pain and nausea seeing her shattered face, her charming smile blown apart by shrapnel. The shock was such that he was stunned, not knowing what to do or where to go. When the explosions ceased people ran to help, looking for survivors in the ruins.

"Tomás, here, here!" They called out to him.

They found his father under a wooden beam that crushed his body. He had both legs broken and was mangled inside. Still, he was somehow conscious. His voice was very weak and Tomás had to get close to hear his last words.

"Never give up. Take care of your mother and tell her I love her."

"Father, father!" He called between tears, but his pale face and frozen gaze indicated his soul had departed, leaving the lifeless body empty.

RICHARD REFUSED TO believe what he had heard, he decided to leave Mrs. Basilisa in the Malaga cathedral and return to Almeria. When he arrived in the city he saw it had become a battlefield, craters, collapsed houses and streets blocked by rubble. Once the bombing ended people immediately organized themselves to search for survivors and assist the wounded. He asked people in the market area, but no one remembered seeing Tomás. The shock was widespread, many seemed absentminded, others wandered lost, most were looking for family and friends. He helped organize rescue efforts: rows of people to remove debris, moments of silence to hear if there were people trapped in the ruins. The whole city mobilized in solidarity to help each other. Private cars to transport the injured. Lost children were taken to the School of the Company of Mary, where they would be cared for while waiting for a family member to pick them up. When the efforts were organized he continued looking for Tomás. He scoured the city from end to end until finally someone told him they had seen him.

"Are you sure it was Tomás García?" He still didn't believe it. "Are you sure?"

The man nodded and the sky opened up for Beckenbauer, he clung to the idea of finding him safe and sound. Finally he found him embracing his father's corpse. He was devastated, crying in pain and anger.

"Tomás, come with me, we have to go." He held out his hand to him.

"Look, look what you've done, this is all your fault..." Tears of grief mixed with anger.

"You can't stay here." He kept holding out his hand. "I took your mother to Malaga."

"I said get out!"

With all the sorrow in his heart Richard left, to return again to the cathedral where refugees were arriving from all over Andalusia. From the very instant he refused to follow Commander Uli's orders, his past in Germany was erased, the only family he had left was here, Tomás and his mother. At least he would make sure Mrs. Basi was well. He would try to atone for his sins, deceived and led by arrogance, he betrayed those who loved him. The commander used his reports to gather information that was later sent to the rebel side, reaching General Franco's hands. That way they knew how the city's defenses were constituted. Malaga was overwhelmed by the huge number of people wandering its streets with their meager belongings, tired and hungry with nowhere to go. No one imagined the African army along with the Italians would attack the city. The defense was in the hands of civilians, militiamen armed with some rifles, pistols and hunting shotguns. They waited in vain for weapons, ammunition, air support and the sending of troops from Valencia. When Richard was arriving in the city chaos broke out, people fled en masse down the road toward Almeria to continue to Murcia. The endless columns of people marching on foot blocked the road. He honked the Renault's horn and gestured with his hands for people to move aside, but barely advanced a few meters. He turned around, and picked up the smaller children and a woman carrying a baby. Juan Pedro, Tomás's cousin, and his wife with their newborn baby in her arms were among the crowd, they saw him from afar, but although they shouted calling him he couldn't hear or see them in all that noise and people.

In early February, Francoist troops were at the gates of Malaga, that's when the exodus of thousands of people by road to Almeria began. African troops, legionnaires and Italian fascists were entering the city. People took what little they had, what they could carry, and abandoned their homes. More than fifty thousand women and children refugees had concentrated in the Malaga cathedral from all the surrounding villages. Captured men were trucked to cemeteries where they were shot.

Some two thousand poorly armed Republican militiamen with rifles tried to confront a professional army equipped with mechanized artillery and over thirty thousand soldiers. A squadron of the Condor Legion also accompanied them by air.

To make matters worse, the Republican battalions were divided by their affiliation to different parties: socialist, anarchist, communist battalions and each interpreted orders their own way. The Nazi bombings of the city were continuous, sowing chaos and terror among the population, over two hundred and fifty deaths from bombs were recorded.

Pepe Baena led a militia company that tried to stop the fascist advance from one of the bunkers. The population of Malaga was being driven mad by the continuous bombings. The nights tended to be long and dark, in the areas of the city that still had electricity, they were forced to cut it due to the constant air raid alarms. Not only did they have to watch out for bombs, snipers were positioned on distant rooftops, shooting at anything that moved. It is estimated that during those months there were around a hundred raids by German and Italian bombers. Most of the population, women and children, left Malaga heading to Almeria on foot along the road. Those who left earlier and were up front avoided the bombings, but were often strafed by fighter planes. The pace of the elderly and children was slow, they barely had anything to eat, they chewed on sugar cane to survive.

On the third day of walking, in the morning, María del Rosario stopped to rest and breastfeed her newborn. She was weak, she had given birth eight days earlier. When Juan Pedro learned that

Nationalist troops were approaching, he decided to abandon the city as soon as possible. He carried a bundle on his back, with blankets to spend the night and an old suitcase, where they kept their meager belongings. The little food they had, two loaves of bread and a piece of bacon, was gone. María couldn't make too much effort, she got dizzy walking but didn't want to stop and rest and fall behind. On the fourth day she got up frozen, trembling and feverish, still she got to her feet staggering and they continued on.

"We'll rest under that bridge." Juan Pedro pointed to the stone viaduct up ahead. "How are you feeling?"

Her frail appearance, dry, colorless lips, clouded gaze. She said nothing, she kept walking leaning on her husband's arm. The baby hadn't cried all morning. Sheltered under the old bridge many families rested while an endless line of refugees crossed in front. Tired people, old and sick, lost gazes not understanding what had happened, how their world had collapsed. A family prepared breadcrumbs in the pan over the embers and seeing Juan Pedro's sick wife, they offered her some in a paper cone.

"Wait for me here, I'm going down for water to the stream." She had sat on the ground, leaning against the granite wall.

He took the empty wine bottle, removed the cork and went to the bank to fill it. The small stream ran parallel to the road and disappeared into the distance. The water was clear, crystalline. He submerged the transparent glass bottle and filled it. He was so thirsty he almost drank it all in one gulp, he refilled it and when he went to put the stopper he seemed to see some dirt inside. The current now flowed turbid, the orangey brown tone similar to iron oxide and suddenly turned blood red. He returned frightened to his wife. María del Rosario bared her pale, languid breast and put it in the baby's mouth. She felt the cold lips of death. Looking at the lifeless body of the child, she went mad, she began a mute cry, her voice was gone and she cried trying to scream but no sound came out. Juan Pedro held her before she fell unconscious to the ground. She clutched the corpse of the baby to her chest, protecting it so no one would take it from her. The husband abandoned the suitcase leaving it there and picked up his dying wife in his arms. He was very tired and had to stop every few steps to rest. A few hours later corpses began to appear on the roadside ditches. First one every now and then, then he came across dozens, maybe hundreds. Their blood dyed the stream water and the red current disappeared into the distance. The lifeless bodies were whole, in one piece, so he deduced it wasn't from the bombings. He continued on his way, along with the rest of the people who passed covering their children's eyes. The women in mourning made the sign of the cross. The drone of engines was heard and out of nowhere three Fiat Chirris descended. They dove down and began strafing people, who in that area had nowhere to hide. Hundreds of people, women and men with small children in their arms ran terrified. They fell to the ground dead, killed instantly riddled by the rain of lead. Juan Pedro threw himself to the ground on top of his dying wife who still held the baby. Bullets pierced his body from head to toe. María del Rosario lay there looking at the sky, with the corpse of her child and husband on top of her. Those who left first and were up front became prey for the fighter planes; those who left later were massacred by the warships' cannons. Positioned off the coast, with the road in front, firing indiscriminately at the people, just like target practice. The bombardment was lethal, shells were launched from the warships and planes. There were injured women and children, dead strewn on the roadside ditches. Blown apart, with streaks of blood coming out of the holes, from their ears, nose and mouth. Meanwhile the fascist press boasted of having liberated Malaga. There were documentary films about the Italian troops entering the city. Strange dichotomy, the Fascist troops of Mussolini and the Nazi army and air force of Hitler liberating a city by expelling most of its inhabitants. Many who stayed would be jailed and finally shot, there was no peace for the defeated. Anyone who was suspected of being a Red or looking like one, simply disappeared. The road trip along the highway continued to Motril, where the Republican border was located. A two hundred kilometer journey that for the elderly, women and children became a nightmare. As they advanced the bombings increased, unleashing themselves on the civilian population in indiscriminate carnage. A continuous cloud of smoke enveloped the Canarias, Baleares and Almirante Cervera warships. Along the road there were puddles of blood and dismembered bodies, blown to pieces by the explosions. Limbs and torso in one ditch and an arm and head in the other. The horror of Pablo Picasso's Guernica painted in bright red blood. The screams and cries of women and children who came across the mangled corpses of their relatives, siblings, parents and children strewn on the road.

Chapter 25

Rescue Mission

THE JUNKERS REMAINED on the beach, they had put it under the cliffs and camouflaged it with branches. At party headquarters Richard proposed flying to Malaga and getting as many people out of there as possible, for that he needed to inform the authorities to prepare a lit area where he could land.

"Malaga general secretariat speaking." He heard the voice breaking up amid the sound of nearby explosions.

"This is Richard Beckenbauer calling from Almeria, I need you to provide me a place to land."

"The Francoists are entering Malaga, we have evacuation orders, but the rail line has been cut off." The man was desperate.

"I'll touch down tonight at eleven and get everyone I can out of there."

"But are you aware of the danger you're facing? The Condor Legion and the Italian air force control the skies."

"That's why I'll have to fly at night, get me a lit field so I can land."

Tomás García and Pepe Baena received orders to prepare the Eras area, where summer threshing was still done so the Junkers Ju 52 could land there. They had no generators, so they had to scour Malaga asking for as many vehicles, cars and trucks, so their headlights could illuminate the runway. They delimited the four corners with ditches where they mixed straw and diesel, preparing bonfires that would be lit at the right time.

Diane Klum and Michael Horten decided to accompany him when they saw what was happening, the bombing, persecution and massacre of civilians, they decided to take sides by helping however they could. They knew what was at stake by entering a besieged city. They took off at dusk from the Almeria beach and flew at night until reaching the landing area, but they didn't see any lights, the city was dark. For a moment he thought maybe Baena hadn't followed orders; if they didn't provide them an adequate, lit place to land they would end up crashing. They circled while the clock hands slowly reached the agreed upon time, at that moment the makeshift airfield lit up.

"There, there it is." Michael pointed toward the lights.

Richard made a spiraling descent, confirming an easterly wind was blowing. They touched down without incident.

"Okay, we have to make sure the injured, women and children get on first." He gave Diane and Michael instructions.

Doctor Klum was in charge of triage, classifying the people who would go on the first trip according to priorities. Michael helped get the injured on board. Pepe Baena approached Richard.

"You bastard! Crazy German." He said it smiling as he shook his hand.

"We have to hurry, we'll make as many trips as we can. I'll unload in Cartagena and come right back."

Among the crowd, helping an old man up the wooden gangway, he saw Tomás and his heart skipped a beat. They had been waiting for several days for someone to come rescue them, but so far only Richard Beckenbauer had dared to do so. It was necessary to get as many people out of there as possible and especially Tomás's mother who had to travel to France to request aid. The two stood still looking at each other for an instant.

"Anger and fear clouded my vision, but now I can see you again." Tomás apologized with the words of a poet.

José Luís Baena interrupted the reunion, he positioned himself between them keeping them apart.

"We have to stand united, we must fight together." Baena hugged them both at the same time. "Allow me to fight by your side comrades."

Pepe Baena was not a man of words, nor one to show affection, so they both understood these were his apologies for having humiliated them.

"What you've done, stealing that plane from the Nazis, risking your life to save my people, makes you one of ours." Tomás shook his hand firmly and hugged him in front of everyone present.

Tomás spoke to the crowd, he told them not to worry, that justice and truth would prevail. That reinforcements would arrive, that they had to temporarily depart to Murcia and Valencia, but that as soon as the weapons arrived from Russia they would return home.

"We have to take up arms, fight to defend freedom. Fight so that justice and truth prevail. We'll speak with the French government."

He made five trips that night, on the last one Tomás's mother boarded, she had to meet with Dolores Ibarruri in Paris. They had a planned meeting with French ministers, to discuss the situation of the Republic, the repeated noncompliance by the Italians and Germans with the non-intervention treaty. When all passengers were on board, they lit up the vehicles and Richard slammed the throttle, the runway was full of potholes and at the end there was a grove, every time he gained speed he felt they wouldn't make it and end up smashed against the pines. Tomás occupied the co-pilot seat, that gave him some reassurance, when he was by his side he felt capable of doing anything. They both pulled hard on the controls to lift the nose in time and cleared them by just inches, grazing the treetops. The sky began to change color, dawn was breaking and with first light the Italian Chirri fighter planes took off from the Seville airport. They climbed as high as possible, trying to camouflage themselves among the clouds. Diane tended to the wounded, while Michael looked out the window praying no enemy planes would appear.

"There's a fighter squadron at eight o'clock." Michael informed them.

"Tell the people to hold on tight to whatever they can, it's going to be a bumpy flight."

The smoke tracer bullets started whizzing by in front of them. When the Fiats caught up to them, Richard and Tomás performed all the evasive maneuvers they had practiced with their planes. But the Junkers was too slow and heavy, they didn't stand a chance.

"We have to hold on a little longer, the Chato and Mosca will be here soon." Tomás peered at the sky, praying to see them appear.

"The left engine is on fire." Michael Horten informed them.

A machine gun burst came through the windshield, the bullets crackled ricocheting off the metal structure. When Richard turned he saw Horten dead. Engine grease was coming into the cabin splattering Tomás's face, he wiped it with his hands. Then they saw twenty-four Republican fighter planes appear, the Polikarpov I-15 Chato and Polikarpov I-16 Mosca. They were far superior planes to the Fiat Chirris, so the Francoists immediately retreated, still they lost several aircraft before leaving Republican airspace. The plane was hit by a machine gun burst from tail to nose, several people were injured, although Michael Horten got the worst of it. Diane rushed to assist him, she took him in her arms, he was still alive and conscious, although he was mangled, the exit holes in his back were huge.

"Did we make it?" He asked in a faint voice, worried about the people they were carrying in the plane.

"Yes, we gave them the slip and our fighters are pounding them."

"I'm glad about what we did, it's the only good thing I've done in my whole life."

"You did very well, we saved many people."

He died with a smile on his face. Diane closed his eyes and looked at the pilots, she realized things didn't look good. Tomás felt the sting of a wasp on his leg.

"You've been hit." Diane took off her seatbelt and put it on as a tourniquet.

The engines were on fire, they were rapidly losing altitude, they were going down into the sea. Oddly what scared Richard most wasn't crashing and dying, it was falling in the middle of the sea and drowning. Since he was a child he'd always had nightmares about drowning. He tried to ditch, to land the plane on the water's surface. They were over three kilometers from shore. With Tomás's help he made a perfect water landing, bellyflopping with the Junkers on the water. It skipped five times and when it lost speed and finally stopped, they were on the beach. In the back there were crying children, but they had made it.

What hurt Tomás most was not the leg wound, he suffered for the people left behind in Malaga that they could no longer rescue. Richard's priority was getting people to safety, they would see later how he might return and help the people escaping the city.

"How are you, can you walk?" He was worried about Tomás.

"It's nothing, just grazed me. I'm sorry about your friend, he was a good man."

AT THAT VERY MOMENT people were being murdered on the Malaga to Almeria road. The massacre was known as the Retreat, some five thousand civilians lost their lives, refugees escaping from the city. The N-340 road goes up from Cadiz to Barcelona. Malaga had been characterized by its labor movement, especially the CNT and the Communist Party. The communists had achieved the first deputy in the province's history, in the February 1936 elections. They called the city Red Malaga. The polarization of the citizenry brought out unusual violence, clashing with the established powers several convents were burned. This was testing Commander Uli Lindemann's patience as he eagerly awaited being allowed to act. Thanks to the action of the labor militias that managed to contain the coup leaders, the province of Malaga remained under Republican control. They were practically isolated from the rest of territories controlled by the government. The only connecting route was the Almeria highway, which was threatened by the Francoist side's warships, plus floods had occurred around Motril, various landslides and mud and rock avalanches had wiped out sections of the asphalt. Due to this, finding themselves cut off, they had to make decisions on their own, often disregarding the Republic's orders. On January 17, 1937 General Queipo de Llano ordered an offensive on the province of Malaga. The troops occupied Marbella, Alhama and surrounding territory, but hardly encountered any Republican resistance, people fled to Malaga and those in charge of the city's defense didn't think the attack would go any further. The Republican authorities dismissed the onslaught and sent no reinforcements. The Italian Blackshirts had nine battalions ready for the attack, a total of some ten thousand soldiers. On the other side the Republic had about twelve thousand militiamen in Malaga, but they only had some eight thousand rifles and scarce ammunition. The final attack began on February 3 entering from Ronda toward the city. Here Francoist troops encountered fierce resistance. Panic spread among the refugees seeing they could get cut off. The Republic ordered the evacuation of the city that same day.

Chapter 26

Narbonne Station

THE NIGHT TRAIN DEPARTED the Barcelona station heading for Narbonne, France, crossing Gerona. Tomás's mother, Mrs. Basi traveled accompanied by Richard Beckenbauer. It was a long journey and not without danger. There were right-wing Spanish secret service agents infiltrated among the passengers, every now and then they would act eliminating selected targets from headquarters in Salamanca. It was a dangerous spy game, any stranger could enter one of the railcar compartments and assassinate someone by slitting their throat. That's why Richard decided to accompany Mrs. Basi, without drawing attention, he preferred to go unnoticed like just another traveler going to France - days later the French government closed the border - for personal reasons. He stayed smoking a cigarette in the hallway, contemplating the night views through the window. While Tomás's mother entered the small compartment with facing bench seats. There were four elderly men, she was the only woman. One of them got up and helped her place her black leather bag on the luggage rack.

"Thank you very much, you are very kind." After those courteous words she sat down opposite him.

"It's nothing. Are you traveling to France or getting off in Gerona?" The man asked with a French accent.

Given the circumstances the question seemed inappropriate, if not impertinent. The other three men remained seated with long faces: the thin, wrinkled one nervously looked at his hands, the one in the black beret pulled down to his eyebrows stared into space through the ceiling and the other fat one with cared for hands tried to sleep. She deduced that one must be a priest, by his bulky physique, delicate hands and very short hair, maybe he had shaved his head to eliminate the tonsure on his crown.

"Giuseppe Bonnaire." He introduced himself with a wave of his hand. "Silk accessory merchant, men's handkerchiefs and women's stockings. I travel constantly back and forth and now with everything in an uproar I have more work than ever."

"Italian name and French surname?" It was clear he was a chatterbox best humored, although she didn't appreciate him mentioning the war as a business opportunity at all.

"My parents' quirks, I'm the curious mix of a Frenchman, an Italian woman and Catalan childhood and nanny. Seller of French products in Spain and vice versa."

The German finished his cigarette while thinking of Tomás, he had stayed in Valencia where he had several important meetings with leaders of the anarchist and communist parties. The steam locomotive let out a long whistle before entering a narrow tunnel. Except in the first class coaches, where the windows had a sliding section, all the others were fixed as one piece of glass and it was partly due to the numerous narrow tunnels where the boiler smoke condensed. Shortly after leaving Barcelona the fine rain turned to sleet, the snowfall was intense, in Gerona the train stopped for longer than usual, the driver debated with the station master about the state of the tracks after the latest weather report. A couple of civil guards in rural service uniform boarded, in grayish green suits, yellow waist sash and patent leather tricorne hats. In this area the civil guard remained loyal to the Republic and it was certainly better to encounter a checkpoint conducted by them, than by militiamen, whichever side you were on, you never knew how it would end up. Despite the intense storm the driver made the decision to continue on to France. Fourteen kilometers from Narbonne the train stopped trapped by the heavy snowfall, a small avalanche of snow overflowing from the hillside had covered the tracks. The passengers became alarmed and the conductor went by informing them of the situation. There was nothing to worry about, as soon as the station master noticed the delay, he would send the Beyer-Garratt snowplow locomotive.

Following the engine was the small wagon with the coal used as fuel, then came the dining car, the sleeper cars, first class coaches and finally second class where Richard and Mrs. Basi were traveling. The civil guard went forward checking documentation and passports from the front to the rear of the train. A tall, thin man dressed in a gray suit and felt hat of the same color, left his first class compartment and walked swiftly putting some distance between himself and the guards. He passed by crossing among the onlookers who came out into the hallway to find out what was happening. Except for Beckenbauer no one noticed the fleeing man.

"I have to get off." The chubby man who looked like a chaplain woke up startled.

"What's going on out there?" Asked the thin, nervous man.

Richard calmly entered the compartment, he sensed the checkpoint was due to the man trying to escape.

"Nothing, there's nothing to worry about." The German reassured Tomás's mother. "It's just a routine check."

When he said that, the fat man made a motion to get up and run away. Richard stopped him by putting a hand on his shoulder, pressing for him to sit back down. You didn't have to be a great observer to notice the disguise, one more of so many clergymen trying to cross into France. As long as he kept his composure everything would be fine, despite his unconvincing cover, he was lucky, the guards' attention, their mission, was something else. The man in the suit reached the rear, opened the door and jumped into the snow.

"Halt civil guard!" The youngest guard shouted from the outer step holding the handle.

The fugitive didn't stop, he tried to escape with difficulty, since his smooth soled dress shoes sank into the snow.

"Halt or I'll shoot!" The civil guard aimed his rifle braced against the railcar.

Two seconds later the blast was heard and the man was struck down like a deer. His hat flew off his head as he fell and rolled in the snow. The silk merchant had looked out the hallway window and upon seeing what happened ran to grab the suitcase he had left on the luggage rack. Richard and Mrs. Basi watched the four terrified men. The only one who remained unfazed was the one in the beret, who kept staring into space. Maybe he was the only one not in disguise, the others were impostors trying to leave the country. The cardboard suitcase slipped from his hands, falling with a thud from above, its contents spilled out. Among the clothes there was gold jewelry and silver flatware. Beckenbauer helped gather it all up.

"Put the luggage back where it was and return to your seat." He spoke to everyone. "Each of us has our own reasons for traveling to France, staying calm there will be no problem."

The snowplow cleared the tracks and with a whistle the locomotive started up again. Once the suited man's corpse was identified, they left it tossed among the pines and got back on the train. The sliding compartment door abruptly opened and the officer who had just shot the fugitive came in asking for documentation. Nerves betrayed the fat man who searched for his passport in his jacket pockets. The guard scrutinized the photo and stamp in detail. The priest couldn't stand the tension and suddenly snapped.

"THAT GENTLEMAN IS A criminal, look in his suitcase." He pointed to merchant Giuseppe Bonnaire.

"That's a lie, shit priest!" The other yelled as the guard drew his gun.

The two agents struggled and chaos broke out inside the small compartment. The fate of the travelers hung by a thread, any of them knew how it would end if detained. They were nothing more than a group of desperate men, each with their petty sins. People trying to escape the war, survive, without taking sides. Most would call them traitors and cowards, but perhaps in a war the only really right thing is individualism, thinking for and by oneself. Getting as far away to safety as possible, while fathers and sons, cousins and brothers kill each other.

"Wait a moment, everyone calm down." Tomás's mother stood up and spoke to them as if they were small children, boys fighting in the schoolyard. "What's in that suitcase is mine, we need it to cover travel expenses. And yes...the father accompanies us."

By showing them her passport they knew it was Mrs. Basi, they had been informed of her trip. The man they had just shot was a spy, a hitman ordered to find Tomás's mother and eliminate her. On this occasion everyone came out unscathed, the guards' orders were to escort Mrs. Basi, get rid of any danger that had gotten on the train. They had no intention of arresting anyone, much less a priest. They could be ordered to do many things, but they were still Christians, they had never missed a Sunday mass. Mission accomplished, that's where their jurisdiction ended, in Narbonne station they would turn around and head back home.

Chapter 27

Meeting in Paris

THEY ENTERED CAFÉ PROCOPE through the back passage off Cours du Commerce Saint-André. Tomás's mother went arm in arm with Beckenbauer. The waiter led them upstairs where Dolores Ibarruri awaited having a mint and lemon balm infusion. Le Procope was the oldest café in Paris, where show business people, authors like Voltaire and Rousseau met, it was the first literary café. It is said that Benjamin Franklin drafted the United States constitution within its walls. There's no need to agree with Dolores Ibarruri's political ideas - La Pasionaria - almost a hundred years later it is very difficult if not impossible to put oneself in the circumstances of the time. That's why far from any political movement, the courage of women who faced the established establishment is admirable. Indoctrinated from childhood in a macho culture and society where the most they could aspire to was to become the wife of a wealthy merchant or the consort of an aristocrat. I'm not even able to imagine where the inner flame comes from that turns an educated girl, seamstress, embroiderer and other domestic chores into a revolutionary leader or aviator, fighting in the skies over Spain in a Polikarpov I-16 fighter.

Dolores Ibarruri was already a mother of six children at twenty-two when she decided she had to do something about the filth and began her political career. She told her husband she had no intention of having more children, nor spending more time sewing, scrubbing or cooking in the kitchen. She would devote her life to defending the rights of the most disadvantaged. Just this act of rebellion, of confronting society already has all my admiration. Daughters or wives of wealthy people who strayed from the path were professionally treated, committed to the psychiatric hospitals of the time. The upset father or husband could sign authorizing admission, as long as he paid the monthly fee the woman would never see the light of day again. Electroshock therapy and lobotomy, brain surgery, were recommended.

Born into a mining family, she was fortunate to be able to study until age fifteen and although she dreamed of being a teacher, she trained in dressmaking and joined the textile workers of the time. This awakened her political interest in defending workers' rights. In 1918 a turbulent Spain was shaken by the working class revolutionary movements. On Easter she published her first article in the newspaper El Minero Vizcaíno and given the dates she used the pseudonym La Pasionaria, a fortuitous name by which she would become popularly known. In 1921 she joined the recently founded Communist Party. Her passionate oratory and defense of the miners during the revolutionary strike and riots in Asturias in 1934 made her a world famous politician. Tomás's mother had known her for many years and they were good friends, that's why they met, to find out firsthand how things were from Malaga to Valencia. To prepare an international aid petition that would allow the Republican government to control the rebels. They were invited to the solidarity rally with the Spanish people at the Winter Velodrome, they listened to Dolores Ibarruri speak next to them on the platform:

Standing firm at the microphone, dressed in black as always with her traditional bun, she spoke addressing the workers of Paris, the democrats of France. She told them how the Spanish Republic was fighting against international fascism. How they were dying in an unequal struggle. She spoke to them of republic and democracy. That of our country and theirs. She made a demand, a request for solidarity with the Spanish Republic, with the certainty that they would understand and be able to help us. The thousands of people who packed the venue stood and applauded. She paused for a few seconds and spoke forcefully again. The rebel military had left the Republican government without the most basic means of defense. But democrats, the entire people had risen up against the fascist coup plotters without regard for the lack of weapons needed to defend themselves. She announced that Hitler's and Mussolini's armies were supporting the rebels, fighting the democratically elected government, massacring the civilian population in indiscriminate bombings of cities. Women and children were being murdered, victims of bombs and shrapnel. She told them the French government had refused to supply weapons for the defense of the Spanish Republic. She appealed to French women. She had not come to ask for their sons and husbands to spill blood for democracy, they were only being asked to petition their government for a change in its non-intervention policy. Armed exclusively with reason and heroism they could not confront rifles, planes and cannons. She paused again, the mournful gesture on her face at what she was about to say, at what was foreseen and no one wanted to hear; that no one should forget that after us would come the others, if the Spanish people were crushed, fascism would spread through Europe like cancer. Perhaps it was the most revealing part of her speech. The war had just begun in Spain and the democratic countries of Europe were already being warned that this was the beginning of World War II:

Help us prevent the defeat of democracy, because the consequence of this defeat would be a new world war, which we all have an interest in preventing and whose first battles are already being fought in our country. For our children and for yours! For peace and against war, demand the borders be opened! Demand the French government fulfill its commitments to the Spanish Republican government! Help us get the weapons we need to defend ourselves! Fascism shall not pass, it shall not pass, it shall not pass!

Paris 1936
Dolores Ibarruri
La Pasionaria

FRANCE, GREAT BRITAIN and the United States refused to lend aid to Spain's democratically elected government. The Madrid government requested the purchase of planes from France, but was denied. The coup rebellion could have been quashed in the early days, but the democratic governments looked the other way, saying it was a civil war in which they should not intervene. They did not object to the intervention of Mussolini's Fascist Italy and Hitler's Nazi Germany. Thus the story of a betrayal was written, turning their backs on the Republic's government and allowing fascists and Nazis to use Spain as a training ground. The policy of non-intervention by the European powers allowed the Italians and Germans to supply Franco with weapons and troops while at the same time preventing the weapons purchased by the Republican government from Russia from crossing the border.

On July 6 Commander Líster attacked the Nationalist troops besieging the city of Madrid. An air force of about two hundred planes was sent. The eleventh division broke through enemy lines and reached Brunete. In the following days other towns were added. In the air battles on the 8th, the Yugoslav pilot Boško Petrović managed to shoot down the first Messerschmitt Bf 109 in history. Francoist troops received reinforcements on the ground and aerial intervention from the Condor Legion, recovering the lost towns. The Republic had to fall back and retreat. The battle resulted in numerous casualties, material and human. Half of the aircraft were lost. About a hundred Republican planes shot down versus the twenty-three lost by the Francoists.

Chapter 29

War in the Sky

AT THE START OF THE Civil War there were only about four hundred planes in Spain. Around one hundred were commercial and of the few military aircraft, many were disassembled or so old they could barely fly. About two hundred aircraft and some one hundred and fifty pilots were left in the hands of the Republican government, while the rebel side had about ninety planes and pilots. Initially and due to the sending of armaments by Italy, some French businessmen and government officials of the Leon Blum administration, sent shipments of new aircraft for the Republic's defense. Approximately one hundred and twenty aircraft were received in total. The Dewoitine 371 fighters and Potez 54 bombers arrived at Prat de Llobregat airport in Barcelona. The FARE, popularly called The Glorious, were the air forces of the Spanish Republic that remained operational between 1936 and 1939. It gained great prestige during the Civil War defending the skies over Madrid. Things later became more complicated due to the increasing intervention of German and Italian pilots and planes. The Glorious gradually lost its luster as its forces dwindled to near extinction at the Battle of the Ebro. It was an unequal fight, the FARE always fought at a numerical disadvantage. At first the battles took place mainly in the Sierra de Madrid and over the Strait, although the old, outdated planes had little if any success preventing the Italian-German airlift that transported Franco's troops from Africa to the mainland. Later the Italian and German bombers arrived in Madrid, first bombing the Getafe and Cuatro Vientos airfields, then doing so in the capital, dropping their bombs on the civilian population. That's when the inferiority of the Republican air forces became apparent. Unexpectedly the tide turned when Stalin authorized the sending of Soviet planes to the Republic. The Polikarpov I-15 and I-16 fighters, the Chato and Mosca, which at the time were the fastest and most modern in the world. Fast bombers like the Tupolev SB-2 Katyushka were also sent. Experienced Russian pilots were incorporated and Spanish pilots were also trained at a secret base in the USSR. Now air superiority over the skies fell to the Republic's government and it was key to the successful defense of Madrid. Patrols of fighters, first the Fiat CR32 Chirris, the Heinkel He 51Bs and later the fast, modern Messerschmitt Bf 109Bs appeared out of nowhere when least expected. They could be attacked at any time, Tomás García and Richard Beckenbauer only had a few seconds to react, to live or die, stay in one piece or streak across the sky in a fireball. Each confrontation was a fight to the death, shoot down the enemy or be shot down yourself. Novice pilots seldom survived the first month of combat. Missions became increasingly dangerous, for every Nationalist plane shot down, two more took its place, while the Republican air force had no replacements, downed aircraft had to be added to those that simply broke down from lack of parts and maintenance. That morning at base only Tomás's Mosca and Richard's Chato were operational.

World War I German Ace Oswald Boelcke published the eight rules for aerial combat:

1 - Try to gain advantage before attacking, keeping the sun at your back, have greater speed and altitude, assess the capabilities of each aircraft and number of attackers. Initiate combat first and by surprise.

2 - Once the attack has begun, carry it through to the end, never retreat, as fleeing makes you an easy target.

3 - Only fire at close range with the enemy framed in the gunsight. Running out of ammo can mean death.

4 - Never lose sight of the opponent, don't be fooled by his tricks.

5 - It is essential to attack the adversary from behind, from the six o'clock position. Opening fire from tail to nose.

6 - If the enemy dives at you, don't try to evade, fly to meet him.

7 - In enemy territory, the exit direction must be memorized in order to return to friendly terrain.

8 - For the Staffel, attack in groups of four or six aircraft, each must select a target, taking care not to have two pilots attack the same opponent.

THE TWO TOOK OFF TO try to stop the Italian and German bombers unloading their deadly cargo on the civilian population. Shortly after takeoff they spotted four black dots in the distance, they were four Savoia Marchetti 79 bombers, escorted by eight Fiat Chirri fighters. Tomás and Beckenbauer gained altitude keeping the sun at their backs so as not to be seen. The planes passed below them. They divided targets, cut throttle and dove down, first attacking the Chirris. Before they could realize what was happening two had been hit. The fighter group, not seeing the attackers, dispersed leaving the bombers unescorted. Tomás and Richard went for them. The Savoia crews spotted them and tried an evasive maneuver quickly descending. Seeing they wouldn't make it they separated and began firing with their rear machine guns, the two skilled fighter pilots stayed out of range. They dove until below the bombers, then aimed for the belly, their weakest area. The Italian airmen in the Savoia Marchettis 79 banked moving the tail to allow the gunners to fire. The four bombers fired their machine guns in unison, producing a very dangerous crossfire. Tracer bullets crisscrossed the sky in all directions and in between were the two small

Russian Polikarovs, looking for a way to shoot down the Italian tri-motors. At Beckenbauer's signal the two climbed gaining maximum altitude then with an Immelmann aerobatic maneuver, they did a half roll with half loop and barrel rolled down firing. They hit two of the bombers but didn't shoot them down and found themselves under crossfire again, disregarding the danger they repeated the maneuver, climbed again and dove on them once more. The Italian pilots were well trained, plus the superior firepower of their planes' defensive machine guns was greater than the two small fighters. Suddenly the Italians made a serious mistake, the planes broke formation and separated so much they couldn't support each other. Instantly Richard and Tomás selected a target getting under their bellies and shot them down. The six CR32s had regrouped and attacked to defend the two remaining Marchetti bombers. Then Tomás ordered a retreat, they had shot down four aircraft, two fighters and two bombers. Two Italian planes broke from the group following them closely. Then Tomás and Richard split up, one banked right the other left. The Chirris followed firing their machine guns. They did a complete circle, now heading straight for each other, the aerobatic maneuver where they crossed just inches apart that they had practiced so many times. The Italian pilots had to stop firing so as not to hit each other and quickly dispersed upon seeing the collision course. Now Tomás had a shot at the Fiat chasing Richard and the German had a shot at the other. They shot them down with the first machine gun burst.

It was nice to be back home, even if home was a damp, foul-smelling barracks. Getting together, having some beers, talking with comrades while playing cards. The worst part of fraternizing was watching them die, disappear from one day to the next. After the first months of war, political ideals didn't weigh as heavily, conversations became more personal. The state of families, wife and daughters or the latest American girlfriend.

"Sorry to interrupt." The young mechanic had a message for Tomás, Richard and Alexey. "You have to report to Malraux's office immediately."

The meeting was to explain that new Russian planes would be arriving. New squadrons of Soviet pilots would also arrive, but more were needed. An agreement had been signed to train new aviators on Russian soil. At a secret base in the Caucasus in Azerbaijan. The three were selected for their skill and Spanish speaking ability.

"I can't abandon my comrades, my country is at war." Tomás objected.

André Malraux explained that the mission was of vital importance, if they didn't train more pilots it would be impossible to win the war. He had already made a decision, he would stay and continue fighting.

"Alright, I understand." Lieutenant Colonel Malraux confirmed.

Once again fate separated them, Richard would travel to eastern Russia to train new pilots, while Tomás García would continue defending the Republic.

The trip to Azerbaijan was long and not without danger, pilots and instructors traveled separately with false passports. Among the young pilots was Dolores Ibarruri's son, Richard took charge of him. The Russian instructors were very experienced, meticulous and strict with training. The training was no game, the exercises performed during maneuvers were truly dangerous. Four Spanish pilots lost their lives in air accidents. Their remains still lie today in forgotten graves in a remote, frigid corner of Azerbaijan where the secret base was located.

THE NEXT ACTION BEGAN on the Aragon front, the goal was to retake Zaragoza for being an important communications hub. It was poorly defended territory like most of the Nationalist front in the area. Failure came from lack of foresight, the International Brigades reached the city, but did not have enough forces to attack, ultimately the battle focused on capturing Belchite. In October and November, Republican aviation focused on bombing military targets like bases and airfields in Zaragoza, Pamplona and Calatayud. One of the most successful missions was the bombing of the Zaragoza airfield. Carried out at dawn, it managed to catch the pilots and ground crews by surprise. Numerous aircraft were destroyed and damaged, including three bombers and three German fighters and another six Fiat CR32s. This paved the way for a new attack by the Republican army, this time attacking Teruel. After two long weeks of fierce combat, the city finally fell into the hands of the Popular army. It was one of the Republic's greatest military successes. The Nationalist side sent a large number of reinforcements, which eventually managed to regain the lost positions. After the defeat, the offensive on the Aragon front continued, the battered and worn Republican army could barely withstand the attack. Francoist aviation, supported by new German and Italian planes and pilots, counterattacked the already depleted Republican aviation, which was now at a numerical disadvantage. The Navarrese requetés penetrated until reaching the Castellón coast, splitting the Republican zone in two.

Chapter 30

Resistance in Malaga

CAVALRY LIEUTENANT General Gonzalo Queipo de Llano took Seville and continued his advance town by town and city by city northward. But most of Malaga's population, loyal to the republic, prevented his advance. Queipo de Llano employed terror tactics against the population, using his continuous radio broadcasts in a psychological war. He gave his troops permission to kill like dogs anyone who opposed his advance. He ordered massive bombings of the city resulting in countless civilian casualties. He bragged of his crimes, mocking into radio microphones:

"I'll sit on a cafe terrace in Malaga, drinking a beer and for each sip ten Republicans will die."

All kinds of people circulated through Malaga's streets, unscrupulous youths and also murderers, convicts released from prisons, who took justice into their own hands. Wearing a tie could be reason enough to kill you. Many good people were murdered for no reason. The manager of a factory or warehouse, accused of crimes committed by his boss. The small businessman who had prospered and ran his own business. There were even landowners who farmed their own land. The first thing was the expropriation of the private to make it public and whoever disagreed with the redistribution was silenced. The landowners, factory owners, wealthy people had left, fleeing the conflict; of course it's not the same reaching the French border on foot and ending up in a refugee camp, as watching the war pass chatting about the situation on a cafe terrace in Monte Carlo, Monaco, Cannes or Nice.

The bombings of the civilian population became reprisals that materialized in mass executions of nationalist sympathizer prisoners. Pepe Baena was in command of a group of anarchists trying to halt the fascist advance in the mountains near the city. A party political secretary tried to encourage the militiamen confronting the fascists in the Malaga mountains.

"There's good news, reinforcements are about to arrive, more troops, weapons and ammunition."

Baena interrupted him.

"What reinforcements or reinforcing, bullshit... What the fuck do we shoot at the Italians, stones with a slingshot? We don't even have any ammo. It seems to me the Valencian communists aren't going to do jack shit."

"Comrade with courage and heart we will prevail. Bombs are nothing where heart abounds."

"Don't give me songs. No matter how many balls we've got, tell me what we shoot with."

They had spent months digging trenches, at war, fighting hand-to-hand against lice. With no military training whatsoever, waiting for ammunition and weapons that never arrived. When the battle began, they couldn't contain the onslaught of the Italian military. The Blackshirts broke through the lines with fire and lead. Baena ordered a retreat, they would go down to the city and try to halt the advance, defending every street inch by inch. Organizing an urban guerrilla war. Pepe knew that every minute, every hour they gained counted, it was vital for the escaping civilian population. They fell back, street by street, until reaching the flour mill where they entrenched themselves. The snipers positioned themselves behind second floor windows and a sharpshooter was posted on the roof. They had little food and scarce ammo. Pepe Baena organized the defense placing each man in the right spot. Diane Klum decided to stay and fight at the flour mill. The fascist army walked right into the ambush. The fifty-three anarchist militiamen opened fire catching the Italians off guard. Dozens fell dead immediately. They tried to fall back, carrying or dragging the wounded by the arms. An armored truck with a machine gun approached down the main avenue. The rooftop sniper aimed at the driver and with an accurate shot hit him in the head. The vehicle kept accelerating out of control, eventually crashing into a wall after leaving the road.

"Contact Valencia headquarters." Baena ordered communications.

The factory phone had a line and he was able to contact Valencia command. They were unaware of the overall situation in Malaga, thinking the Republican army would send reinforcements.

"Lieutenant José Luís Baena speaking, we're surrounded at the flour mill, we need reinforcements." He yelled over the background noise of gunshots.

"We've ordered the evacuation of Malaga. Take the railroad to Cartagena." The voice on the other end of the line was calm, as if it were something trivial.

"What the fuck are you talking about? Service is cut off." He heard silence. "Hello? Listen?"

The call had been cut off. He handed the receiver to the militia comrade and went out of the office yelling.

"Let's go, let's go, a group of five men come with me." Baena led them toward the west side.

They took positions at the windows aiming toward the street in that direction.

"I don't see anyone." The snipers watched the deserted streets.

"Good. They only come in the east side. Let's go back." They ran hunched over, ducking below the windows.

140

Bullets came in shattering the glass, whistling and ricocheting off the walls. They crawled on the dusty plank floor and grouped around the main facade windows.

"Cover us when we go out." He gestured with his hand for the group of five men to follow him. "We'll take advantage now to take their weapons."

After the first wave's retreat, they left the slain soldiers' bodies, weapons and ammo strewn about the street. Pepe's group went outside and in a few seconds gathered as much material as they could.

"Come on, come on, inside." He yelled at the men.

A young man, practically a boy, strayed too far, he now ran to close the gap from one side of the avenue to the other and take cover from the gunfire in the flour mill when he heard a whistle followed by intense pain in his hip and looking down saw blood everywhere. He collapsed screaming in pain. Pepe Baena ran out from the front door, lifted him off the floor and threw him over his shoulder, he ran down the center street as the gunshots intensified, the hissing and ricochets of stray bullets were closer. He ran into the mill.

"I'm going to die, God, I'm dying!" The wounded young man sobbed.

Doctor Diane rushed over to assist him. She lifted his shirt and saw a clean through-and-through hole.

"Don't worry, it's not serious, you'll survive." She held the boy's hand.

With medical attention, in a hospital there would be no problem, but she could do nothing more than bandage the wound. Internal bleeding and infection would end up killing him within hours. Baena positioned the machine gun they had commandeered in one of the windows and opened fire on the soldiers trying to approach. Several fell to the ground riddled with bullets and the rest had no choice but to retreat.

"Cease fire, stop shooting. We have to conserve ammo."

A wisp of white smoke came out of the machine gun's flame dampener, the barrel was glowing red hot. An absolute silence fell, randomly broken by distant shots coming from different parts of the city. Baena ordered communications again to re-contact headquarters.

"Were you able to talk to them?"

"The generals are meeting."

"What do you mean they're meeting?" Baena put his right hand to his head. "What did they tell you?"

"The captain told me to hold on."

"What do you mean hold on? But did he say if reinforcements are on the way?"

"He just said: Hold on and good luck comrades."

He couldn't believe they were leaving them there, not sending troops to defend Malaga. He left the small office with the telephone and returned to the others without saying anything. The first night was long. They took turns standing guard, trying to distribute rest hours. There was no movement in the streets, all that could be heard was the dying young man's agonized breathing. Diane Klum stayed with him until finally in the early morning hours he stopped breathing. The next morning the captain in charge of the Italian Blackshirts spoke to the group of men who had unsuccessfully tried to take the mill. He warned them that this time no one would retreat, they would fight until defeating the enemy. They were far superior in number and better armed. Before initiating combat he requested air support. He got a Savoia Marchetti SM 81 to drop its bombs on the flour mill, although due to strong winds none directly struck it.

"Baena, the general's on the line." Radio communications notified him.

"At your command general, we need reinforcements, we're barricaded in the mill."

There was a heated argument, the two ended up shouting until finally Pepe Baena slammed down the phone.

142

"Cowardly military, sold out communists..." He ranted loudly.

They weren't going to send reinforcements, the order was to get out of there, abandon the city. Still Baena knew his sacrifice hadn't been in vain, they had delayed the Italian advance nearly twenty-four hours, very precious time for the people escaping by road toward Almeria.

The only escape route from the death trap was on the north corner, but an Italian Fiat L3/33 Veloce tank, armed with two machine guns, one 6.5mm and the other 8mm, blocked their path.

"We have to catch them by surprise, as soon as I clear the way get the fuck out of here." Baena gave instructions to the small group that had resisted at the flour mill, including Doctor Diane Klum.

His plan consisted of using an old pickup truck as a battering ram, crashing it into the side of the tank. He undoubtedly knew it was a suicide mission, but was also aware it was the only way to give his companions a chance to escape. The open bed Peugeot 201 was at the top of the narrow rear street. Pepe Baena went out one of the lower windows and crawled until reaching the vehicle. Once in the cab he mentally prepared himself for what he was about to do, best not to think too much about it he told himself. He released the emergency brake and the Peugeot pickup began rolling downhill slowly gaining speed. He put it in second gear and kept his foot on the clutch. The engine was off, as that would have alerted the Fiat L3/33 Veloce crew. It would gain momentum until a few meters away, then in gear with the gas pedal floored, the engine would start up increasing the force of the collision. The security provided by the L3/33 made them overconfident, only watching the mill's facade, unloading intermittent machine gun bursts whenever they sensed movement. The speedometer's red needle was at sixty and at that moment about ten meters from the armored vehicle he released the clutch, the Peugeot 201 engine roared expelling a cloud of black smoke behind it. Baena gripped the steering wheel with all his might. When the Fiat L3/33 Veloce gunner noticed what was barreling toward him, he only had time to yell. The thunderous crash of metal on metal was heard clear across the city. Diane left the factory with the survivors, most of them variously wounded. Passing the accident site, she saw the broken glass, the impact had fused the two vehicles into a huge twisted mess of metal. The fuel and engine oil ignited. A few meters ahead lay Pepe Baena's body, bloody, sprawled on the ground. Despite his heroic sacrifice it was all in vain, they were captured shortly after. By then the entire city was taken and they didn't stand a chance of escaping. Diane Klum was deported, first taken to prison and later sent to the Mauthausen concentration camp where she was admitted on October 31, 1940. When the camp was liberated she was not among the survivors.

ONCE THE REPUBLICAN zone was split in two, General Franco ordered an advance to defeat and capture the combatants still resisting. Unexpectedly they encountered a reorganized Republican force, with the arrival of new Soviet weaponry. The Republic's air force received ninety-nine new Supermosca fighter planes and achieved great success in defense, three squadrons of Polikarpov I-16s shot down twenty-two Italian aircraft.

Chapter 31

500 Nights at the Hotel Florida

THE MALRAUX SQUADRON moved to Barajas Airport in Madrid and the pilots were housed at the Hotel Florida, where the photographers and press of the time were also located. The building had been designed and built in white marble in 1922 by architect Antonio Palacios. It was a short distance from the front and was often a target for shells fired by Franco's troops. Some war correspondents like Geoffrey Cox of the News Chronicle preferred to stay on Gran Vía, living in the Florida was too dangerous. At least thirty shells hit the building. But it was the place to be if you wanted firsthand information. Matthews wrote: "It was the place to be." "Two Wars and More to Come". New York 1938. Outside was the war and inside was madness: Women coming and going from the rooms, sometimes laughing and other times crying accompanied by the waiters. Every night writers, journalists and pilots gathered in its courtyard to share alcohol and stories of what they had seen at the front. Ernest Hemingway, Mikhail Koltsov of Pravda, Henry Buckley of The Daily Telegraph, the Pole Ksawery Pruszynski of Wiadomości Literackie magazine, Geoffrey Cox of News Chronicle and Herbert L. Matthews of The New York Times, they were all part of this unique community. People constantly came and went through its two hundred rooms. And the incessant clacking of typewriters could be heard in the hallways, leaving some of the best chronicles of life in a besieged city. From room 109, Ernest Hemingway's compulsively typing mixed with the aroma of the stews prepared by his roommate, the American bullfighter Franklin.

Your wingman who flew behind you for protection, confusing the enemy and luring them into traps was called your punto or shadow. Tomás was usually Richard's shadow, although in Esquadrilla España's early days, the missions were diverse and the pilots were versatile, flying different fighter or bombing missions changing the squadron's configuration. When they had different shifts or assignments they could go days or even weeks without seeing each other. But the hardest part had been the separation, due to Richard's trip to the USSR, the long waits without news, knowing the other was risking his life up there, flying across skies on the other side of the world. When they finally met that night in the courtyard of the Hotel Florida, Tomás could not contain his emotions. Luckily the darkness accompanied by several bottles of whiskey and the frolicking of two prostitutes prevented anyone from noticing. Ernest Hemingway was semi-unconscious, but they didn't dare take the bottle from his hands. Hemingway's enormous reserve of food and whiskey stored in his room was famous. "What you can drink today, don't save for tomorrow."

Without making any noise they went up to the room where they passionately kissed. Richard pushed Tomás onto his back on the bed then jumped on top of him, unbuttoning his shirt and hurriedly removing the rest of his clothes. It was very difficult to have time alone, they hadn't seen each other for months, hadn't touched each other. Now that they were finally together, they were always under the watchful eyes of strangers. Although some knew their secret, making it public would be frowned upon, at that time they were considered sinners by men of faith and sick by science. Anything done with so much affection and love cannot be ill-regarded by God. Intellectuals like André Malraux didn't care what anyone did in their bed. After the squadron was formed he told them once:

"I want you on your feet and ready for combat first thing in the morning, what each of you does at night is your own business."

The door opened and the light came on, framed by the hallway behind, Ernest Hemingway stood in the doorway. He watched the naked entwined bodies of Tomás and Richard for a few seconds. He raised the whiskey bottle in a kind of cordial greeting and left without saying anything.

With the first light of dawn came the bombing, people ran from the rooms facing the front facade seeking refuge in the interior area. Half naked people, drowsy correspondents and young girls in their underwear. The reality or perhaps the absurdity of war. Once the rain of shells ceased everyone went back to what they were doing, the prostitutes to the street and the rest to scrounge breakfast. Upon returning to his room, Hemingway discovered a jar of jam was missing from his ample pantry. The fuss he made was tremendous, some say World War II began because of the stolen jam. He turned the whole Florida upside down, eventually finding the empty jar in John Dos Passos's room. In bed was Martha Gellhorn, with whom Hemingway was having a romantic affair. How Gellhorn slept with him that night and that same morning appeared sleeping in Dos Passos's bed was none of his business. The only relevant thing was finding out who stole his jam. John and Ernest had been friends and rivals for years, competing in the literary world and also in the suburbs' taverns for the favors of a dark-skinned Gypsy woman. They say that same day Hemingway had Dos Passos's translator arrested, and that was what broke their friendship, but the truth is Ernest refused to speak to John over the jam incident. It's unclear whether it was because of that, that he took the relationship more seriously: Ernest Hemingway married Martha Gellhorn years later.

It was a warm night, the writers, journalists, photographers and Republican officers who had made the Florida their home, brought sofas, armchairs and even mattresses out to the courtyard. In the early evening hours the uproar was huge, everyone discussed what had happened during the day. Tomás García and Richard Beckenbauer recounted the mission they had just returned from. The escort of Katyusha bombers on a mission to destroy a bridge to halt the Nationalist advance. The Francoist troops had a secret fighter plane base hidden among the forests, ready to defend the roads. The only person who knew where they hid was a local shepherd. He couldn't read or write, much less interpret a topographic map, so they had to take him on one of the Tupolev SB-2 Katyushas so he could point out by visual orientation where the enemy aircraft was hiding in the woods.

"Wow! That's a fantastic story." - Sefton Delmer of the Daily Express passed them the wine bottle, inviting them to a drink while asking them to continue the account.

"But what the hell is this?" - Richard's eyes opened wide to look at the bottle, savoring the nectar on his lips. "Where did this wine come from?"

They were used to drinking cheap beer and jug wine, this was neither, possibly the best wine they had tasted in their lives.

"I have my contacts." - And he took out another identical bottle he had hidden under the pillow he was leaning against.

Sefton had the bathroom of his room filled ceiling-high with wine bottles, and this was no ordinary rotgut. He had traded it with four young anarchists for a few dollars and some chocolate bars. They had stolen it from the cellars of the Royal Palace. It had belonged to Charles III the Politician, Charles IV the Hunter, Ferdinand VII the Desired, Joseph I Pepe Bottle - he made good work of them - Isabel II the Chaste Queen, Alfonso XII the Peacemaker, and Alphonse XIII the African, and now Spanish anarchists, English photographers, French novelists, American journalists and the German pilot were guzzling it straight from the bottle. After toasting the good taste in wine of the old Spanish monarchs, they continued recounting their latest mission. The man had never flown in his life and started feeling queasy as soon as they took off. His pale face was disconcerting, he had never seen the world from above. He couldn't get his bearings. The mission commander ordered them down, finally the man realized where they were and pointed to the woods where the Fiat CR32 Chirris were hiding. The mission was a success, they destroyed all the planes before they could take off and then with no one to stop them they were able to bomb the bridge. Sefton took out a notebook and pencil from his shirt pocket and jotted down some notes.

Around midnight, a young lady came screaming out of room 109. Apparently she had had some kind of sexual encounter a few days earlier and thought it was the beginning of something more serious. On her way home she asked her husband, an infantry captain, for a divorce. When the woman presented herself to Hemingway he didn't even remember her name. The captain, with a severe case of cuckold's horns, had followed his wife to the Florida and with all the scandal it wasn't long before he found her. He ran into her in the hallway, after calling her an adulteress and sending her home, he pulled out his service pistol and entered the room.

"Hands up you son of a bitch." - He snapped pointing at the shape moving under the sheets.

He yanked it back and found Richard and Tomás naked.

"I think you have the wrong room. Send any complaints about women to the writer in 109." - Tomás said upon seeing the disturbed look on the soldier's face.

Hemingway, who was listening behind the door, carefully stepped out into the hallway, barefoot, in a sleeveless undershirt and knee-length boxer shorts. It didn't seem like a good time to offer explanations, better to flee than regret misfortunes. The door to the Capas' room was ajar. He went in and bolted the lock. Robert Capa the renowned photographer who had covered a thousand battles, was an invention of two young people, a couple from Budapest. Both were good photographers, but no newspaper wanted to buy the reports of two unknown Hungarians. So between Gerda Taro and Endre Ernö Friedmann they invented the character of the seasoned war correspondent Robert Capa. There was no one there, the bed was unmade and the light on, then he heard the bathroom lock click, he grabbed Gerda's robe and put it on before they came out. His appearance was beyond ridiculous. The two young people emerged with a still-wet photograph in their hands. They used the bathroom as a darkroom.

"Look at this photo, Ernest. What do you think?" - Gerda asked, not paying much attention to his looks, accustomed to his predicaments.

Ernest Hemingway took the photo in his hands, which showed a militiaman at the exact moment he was gunned down: Knees bent, about to fall backwards to the ground, arms outstretched like the crucified Jesus and the rifle slipping from his hands. It was a shocking photo.

"How is this possible? The photographer took it in no man's land, on the other side of the trenches, on the side opposite the Republicans... I've also never seen any soldier who after crawling under enemy fire gets up off the ground with clothes so immaculately white... Damn! But isn't that Tomás García?"

The captain pounded on the door and when it opened the Capas appeared, making up a story about a certain American writer who had returned to his country due to a serious syphilis infection. The man left frightened, touching his genitals.

"Let's say we're even, one secret for another." - She said.

She examined the photograph closely. "I like it, despite everything it has more realism and certainty than most things happening in this damned war."

In July, the popular army began a new offensive on the Ebro lines, taking Franco's African troops by surprise they managed to break through the front. In the opinion of many historians, the war policy promoted by the Communist Party to always attack and never take a step back was a terrible mistake. The air force was not ready to repel the onslaught and by the time they managed to reach that sector it was already too late. The Battle of the Ebro continued throughout the summer and autumn of 1938. During that period the Republican side received shipments of new aircraft: Fifty Polikarpov I-16 Mosca, another fifty Polikarpov I-15 Chato and twenty-four Tupolev SB-2 Katyusha bombers.

Chapter 32

War Over the Sea

Two Tupolev SB-2 Katiuska bombers took off from the Murcia base escorted by four Polikarpov I-16 fighters led by Richard Beckenbauer and accompanied by Tomás García Hernández. The mission was to locate the Admiral Scheer battleship from which Commander Uli Lindemann directed bombing missions against the civilian population. To reach the ship, they had to evade the surveillance of the German Messerschmitt BF 109B fighter planes. As soon as they spotted the battleship, the bombers prepared for the attack when suddenly four German fighters appeared out of nowhere. Over the radio, Richard informed the squadron that the lead planes were under attack by a group of Messerschmitts. The Luftwaffe aircraft were the most modern planes in the skies - fast, hard to see due to their small size, and well armed. Commander Lindemann ordered the gunners to open fire with the anti-aircraft cannons and machine guns. Bullets were flying everywhere, from bottom to top and vice versa. Small black clouds from the exploding anti-aircraft shells in the air, lines of smoke and flashes of fire from the tracer rounds.

Richard and Tomás began to make very tight turns that the faster German fighters could not follow. They made a one hundred and eighty degree turn and the two fighter squadrons crossed each other head-on. The Nazis turned right trying to get behind the Polikarpovs. The eight planes circled around each other, trying to get into position behind one another. The wider turning radius of the Russian planes allowed them to close in second by second until they were in the Germans' tails. Richard and Tomás' plan was to continue turning as tightly as possible to gain ground on the Messerschmitts. They had to secure their target before opening fire since the voracious machine guns on the fighters burned through ammunition in just seconds. Realizing the situation, the commander of the German squadron ordered them to disengage. That was his first mistake - he had violated one of the eight rules of aerial combat drafted by their compatriot Oswald Boelcke during the First World War.

One of the Messerschmitts broke away from the group, climbing to gain altitude. Tomás went after it while the rest of the Republican planes continued chasing the other three. Beckenbauer positioned himself six o'clock behind the Nazi pilot and took him down with the first machine gun burst. After shooting down the first Messerschmitt, the others became jittery, weaving randomly from side to side trying to shake the little Russian fighters off their tails. The anti-aircraft fire from the battleship ceased so as not to shoot down their own planes. Commander Uli was furious and kept shouting for the machine guns to keep firing, but the gunners refused.

- Get the hell out of here, dumbass! - He pushed the soldier away and manned the quad-mount Flakvierling 38 anti-aircraft gun himself.

He fired angrily, cursing ceaselessly. It was nearly impossible to hit the small Russian planes. He then focused on the bombers. The Tupolev SB-2 Katiuskas approached to drop their bombs and the commander clipped one of them, riddling its wing with holes.

- COME HERE, YOU BASTARDS! - He fired all four barrels of the Flakvierling 38.

They released their bombs on the Admiral Scheer battleship with several direct hits on the bridge, and Richard could almost picture Commander Uli Lindemann's face just before being blown to bits. Tomás' Mosca approached Beckenbauer's plane, dipping his wings laughing. It was then that Richard realized Tomás' Polikarpov I-16 had been hit. Oil and black smoke were coming from the engine.

They reached the coast but were still in enemy territory. The German's engine died and he couldn't find anywhere to attempt an emergency landing.

- Head back to base, I'll manage on my own - he told Tomás over the radio.

- We'll take her down together.

- That's not a suggestion - his tone was dry and firm - Return to base, that's an order.

There was radio silence. Tomás gained altitude and stayed six o'clock behind him. Richard's plane was badly damaged with the landing gear shot, a wing half ripped off, and the engine seized up. He couldn't find a suitable place to land, or rather, to crash his I-16 in a controlled fashion. He was losing altitude and airspeed so he had to eject. Tomás watched him land safely by parachute and also noticed a fascist patrol that had seen him go down and were headed his way.

The two soldiers standing guard on the nearby bridge spotted the burning plane and the German ejecting. Beckenbauer hit the ground hard, injuring his leg so he couldn't run. He headed into the scrubland, amidst the rock roses, tall broom and holm oaks. The soldiers started shooting - their intentions were clear, they had orders to take no prisoners. They were going to kill him any second. Each step sent a jolt of searing pain up his leg. He couldn't escape so he lay flat on his stomach. Bullets whizzed by over his head.

Tomás' Polikarpov came out of the clouds, diving at high speed before leveling off just above the ground. When he had them in his sights he opened fire, cutting down the two fascists. Richard got to his feet and watched as he gained altitude before ejecting himself.

- You're completely insane, you could have gotten yourself killed - Richard admonished him.

- I wasn't going to leave you alone. Besides, I didn't have enough fuel left to make it back to base.

Tomás helped him walk and they moved deeper into the mountains where the vegetation was extremely dense. It wasn't a forest of trees - the two to three meter high shrubbery consisted mainly of kermes oak and broom. To the north of the old ruins was a small meadow where thyme had taken over the grassland. A bit lower they found a spring with crystal clear water bubbling up between yellowish boulders. The surrounding soil was clay. Tomás knelt and took a drink of water, then formed a crude clay cup which he baked near the fire. He went back for more water and gave Richard a drink, cleaning and re-bandaging his wound. He noticed he had developed a slight fever. If the infection spread to his blood he could die of septicemia in less than a week.

Tomás spent the rest of the day gathering wild fruits and rigging snares from his bootlaces to trap partridges and rabbits. For three days and nights he never left Richard's side as he battled between life and death, babbling incoherently and groaning continuously. He made sure he stayed warm, wrapping him up and lying beside him. He prepared herbal infusions of mint, lime blossom and rosemary ointments to disinfect the wounds. He had learned a lot watching his mother. The third night was especially long and cold. Tomás remained awake, giving Richard warmth and keeping the small fire going. This was the turning point - Beckenbauer hovered between life and death all night, even stopping breathing for short periods. The next morning he regained consciousness and managed some soup made from wild oats and the roasted carcass of a partridge.

- Thank you for taking care of me - his voice was weak and he fell back asleep, exhausted by the fever.

Tomás kissed him on the forehead and left the shelter in search of water. He crossed the meadow dotted with small blooming thyme plants. The sun shone brightly overhead as the clouds raced by at great speed. Here on the ground, nestled between the mountains, the wind did not reach them - a crystal bubble isolated from the rest of the world, far from the tempest of war. Tomás thought he could live happily here without needing anything else. We waste so much time in life, working towards a better car, a bigger house, and forget what really matters has no price - family, friendship and love. What good is all the gold in the world if you don't have your loved one by your side?

They lived in the ancient ruins isolated from the world for six weeks.

- We have to go back - Richard said that night as they ate roasted rabbit - We have to keep fighting.

Tomás looked thoughtful. He knew sooner or later they'd have to return. They'd been lucky so far but couldn't stay hidden forever. He also realized what going back meant - the war was practically lost.

- We can cross over into France - Tomás' muted tone and the look of a lover.

- You know very well this won't end in Spain - There was a long silence - If we don't stop the Nazis here, they will spread throughout the world.

His mind was made up. They would head back at dawn. Return to the fight. They spent their last night in an embrace, two lovers gazing at a photograph - millions of tiny lights in the sky, casually veiled by the occasional shooting star.

The attrition of Republican air forces during the Battle of the Ebro was brutal. The FARE had lost over one hundred and twenty aircraft and the survivors were in very poor shape. The defeat at the Ebro sealed the government's fate, yet in December the Republican Air Forces of Spain attempted another daring surprise attack on La Cenia, the air base used by the Condor Legion. They destroyed seven of the new Messerschmitt Bf 109E fighters that had arrived from Germany.

In retreat, falling back towards defeat, the attempt was to evacuate the wounded to Madrid. The trucks were packed and Gerda Taro, who had covered the battle extensively in photographs, had no choice but to ride outside hanging onto the running board. Not even reporters were safe - invading troops arriving at the front had an unfortunate tendency of shooting first and asking questions later. Exhaustion coupled with the poor road conditions caused Gerda to slip and fall under the wheels of an armored carrier. Endre Ernö Friedmann received a terse telegram at the Hotel Florida informing him of Taro's death. A part of Robert Capa had died and what remained was not the same.

By the time the Catalonia Offensive began in winter 1939, the FARE was greatly weakened and outmatched from the start. The constant bombing of Republican airfields in the area was relentless. Five planes were destroyed in Figueres and it was much worse in Vilajuïga - thirty-five aircraft in total, Katiuska bombers, Chato and Mosca fighters. By late March, the central front collapsed and after the loss of Catalonia, the remaining provincial capitals still resisting began falling one by one. The war would officially end on April 1st.

In memory of

Tomás García Hernández and Richard Beckenbauer

Tomás García Hernández was shot down on March 4, 1939. His plane cut across the flaming sky in a deadly arc, briefly turning him into a shooting star.

Richard Beckenbauer was hit that same day. He managed to eject and save his life. Captured by nationalist troops, handed over to the Germans days later, transferred to Berlin as a prisoner of war, accused of high treason against his homeland, and executed on October 31.

Epilogue

I've always enjoyed spending a few summer days exploring the Almería coast, visiting small towns, walking the arid, semi-desert landscape, and swimming in hidden coves. There is beauty in the dusty roads that seem untouched for centuries, the turquoise blue sea and its small coves wrapped in eroded white sandstone cliffs carved into unexpected shapes and figures. Mercedes, a friend who scolded me every time she saw me buy a bottle of water, accompanied me. We would pitch the tent near the car anywhere - in the 90s you could still do that - secluded, and take it down at first light. Then on the terrace of a small bar in Rodalquilar village, with just two tables, we'd have coffee with milk and toasted bread. Although we had visited the surrounding beaches and coves, I didn't know the history of the town. That day we walked to Cala San Pedro, where there is a small castle of the same name. We hardly carried any water, because my companion thought it absurd to spend money on a liquid that falls from the sky. I went for a good swim and when I climbed back up the hill I started having terrible pain in my side. I collapsed on the ground dizzy with pain, vomiting. Two young nudist hippies brought me down to the beach where a boat took me to the town of Las Negras and from there an ambulance to the hospital. In total, almost three hours of agony before they gave me a sedative. Luckily it wasn't serious - kidney stones from dehydration. The next morning I felt battered. While having breakfast on the terrace I figured I'd take it easy that day. I asked Juan Pedro, the bar owner, if there was anything interesting to see in town. That's when he told me about the mines.

I visited the mines and the Volcano House museum and became more intrigued when I saw photos of high-ranking SS officers in the same place. In 1940 the mines were nationalized to extract gold to replenish the Bank of Spain's reserves, which had been used by the Republic to purchase armaments from the Soviets - hence the legend of Moscow's gold. The mines were ultimately closed due to low profitability. With rising gold prices, there is talk they may reopen in the near future, although the area is now a protected natural park incompatible with mining. Estimates are of gold reserves around three tonnes in Rodalquilar.

I asked Juan Pedro to tell me more and he introduced me to his grandfather. At ninety years old he vividly recalled everything that had happened. He had known Tomás García Hernández and Richard Beckenbauer personally. José Luís, he said his name was, better known as Pepe Baena. Captured in Malaga after an accident, imprisoned, nearly executed several times, finally released in 1950.

FIRST I WANT TO APOLOGIZE for my lack of historical background on the period of the Civil War. I have been researching for years and the more I delve into specific aspects of the conflict, the more I realize its extreme complexity - the thousands of different versions, the hundreds of relevant characters forgotten in oblivion. In this novel, dedicated to the international pilots who flew in support of the Republic, I came across the incredible stories of Russian pilots who fought in Spain against the Nazis and upon returning to their country were persecuted, imprisoned and many of them finally executed by Joseph Stalin. I learned about Squadron España, created and led by the pilot and writer André Malraux. In his novels he blurs the line between fiction and the real-life adventures he experienced.

Georges-André Malraux was born in Paris on November 3, 1901 and stood out as a writer and politician in the second third of the 20th century. As a child his father abandoned the family, remarried, and eventually committed suicide. Despite growing up in a well-off family, he recalled his childhood with resentment. Self-taught, after dropping out of school at 18, he moved to Paris. At 20 he self-published his first book, Paper Moons, a fantastic tale. At the time he made a living buying and selling rare books. He married Clara Goldsmidt, descendant of Jews of German origin, in 1921. He invested her wedding dowry in a Mexican mining company that soon went bankrupt. As he was interested in archeology he decided to go to Saigon with the aim of making money by stealing artwork from the Banteay Srei temple. They were discovered and detained by the authorities, but the trip served him to write his third novel. This is when he became aware of the situation of the native population under colonial rule, the plundering. Working at a newspaper critical of the government's actions, he began to awaken his commitment to society.

In 1936 Malraux made himself available to the Republican government. Thanks to his numerous contacts and friendships in the French Air Ministry, he managed to purchase fighter planes and bombers. When the aircraft arrived in Spain, he hired private pilots and formed Squadron España. Without even having done military service, he was appointed lieutenant colonel, thus giving the squadron official status. They were among the first to defend Spanish skies. Later they would join the conventional army and the group would take its founder's name, Malraux Squadron. While aiding the civilian population escaping from Malaga, all their remaining aircraft were shot down. From then on he would devote all his energy to fundraising abroad for the Republic's defense.

Antoine de Saint-Exupery

Antoine Marie Jean-Baptiste Roger Count of Saint-Exupery was born in Lyon. After failing naval school, he took advantage of required military service in Strasbourg to become an aviator. He later worked as a pilot delivering mail between Toulouse and Senegal. His early novels revolve around his experiences as an aviator. After the failure of his Aeropostal Argentina venture, he turned to journalism, though he continued flying as a test pilot. At the start of World War II, he was mobilized by the army to an aerial reconnaissance squadron. Despite already being a famous writer, he wanted to continue fighting the Nazis and his twin-engine P-38 Lightning took off on July 31, 1944 at 8:45 AM, never to be seen again.

When I first read The Little Prince - required reading in school - I didn't think much of it. Twenty years later, after reading Antoine de Saint-Exupery's biography, my perspective completely changed. I found in the simplicity of a children's tale much more than meets the eye. Reading about the aviator whose engine fails and makes an emergency landing in the Sahara desert, I picture the harsh reality he faced - lost in the desert, certain to die of dehydration. The night terrors and daytime hallucinations from the heat. A dying man's mind creating a fable, a tale to make you believe the impossible. Did he really see the Little Prince in his delirious hallucinations on the verge of death?

Emergency Maneuvers and Introduction to Aerobatic Flight
Basic airplane controls

The control stick allows pitch motion by raising or lowering the nose around the transverse axis when pushed back and forth. Moving it left or right operates the ailerons, banking the plane around the longitudinal axis by raising one wing and lowering the other. Pressing the rudder pedals activates the tail rudder, causing yaw around the vertical axis - the plane moves left or right like a car. The throttle controls engine power.

Emergency Maneuvers and Introduction to Aerobatic Flight
Angle of Attack

The angle of attack can be described as the position in which the wing cuts through the wind. Pulling back on the stick raises the nose, so air hits a greater surface area of the wing.

Emergency Maneuvers and Introduction to Aerobatic Flight
Stall

There are different types and variables of stalls, notably those due to insufficient airspeed and excessive angle of attack. An accelerated stall is caused by an abrupt increase in angle of attack. Finally, a high-speed stall can occur due to shock waves. An unexpected stall can lead to a crash. Stalling during combat often meant certain death. The plane becomes weightless, motionless in the air for split seconds, enough time to be lined up and shot down by the enemy's machine guns.

Emergency Maneuvers and Introduction to Aerobatic Flight
Stall Speed

Stall speed is generally understood as the speed at which lift decreases to the point that the airplane stops flying. It is also understood that even when maintaining speed, exceeding the maximum angle of attack surpasses the peak of the lift curve - at that point the force of gravity overcomes lift. Due to characteristics like wing surface area, design and weight, each aircraft has a different stall speed. Stalling during a maneuver can be very dangerous, especially when flying low where there is no time to recover. It can be intentionally induced by simply increasing the angle of attack by pulling back on the stick and reducing throttle. This can initiate various aerobatic maneuvers such as a wing-over by banking left or right with the control stick, or a tailslide by pressing the rudder pedals.

Emergency Maneuvers and Introduction to Aerobatic Flight
Tunnel Vision

THE G-FORCES PILOTS endure can drain blood from the head to the feet. With insufficient blood flow reaching the brain, vision darkens, creating a tunnel effect. Peripheral vision is lost and if the forces increase, the tunnel closes completely resulting in total loss of sight and consciousness. Today's fighter pilots wear special suits that automatically inflate, applying pressure to the lower body and preventing blood from draining from the head. Back in the 1930s and 40s, pilots could only rely on training and techniques to remain conscious under these circumstances. We can imagine the situations faced during aerial combat - tunnel vision and blacking out.

Emergency Maneuvers and Introduction to Aerobatic Flight
Wing-Over

This maneuver involves a quarter loop. The greater the speed, the longer it can be sustained. First accelerate in straight flight, then pull up vertically. When the aircraft reaches its ceiling and loses speed, use the rudder pedals to spin it in the same plane, like a car. The rotation ends with a vertical dive. The sequence is: in level flight, apply throttle, pull back on the stick to climb vertically. Before initiating the turn, reduce throttle and apply rudder to spin 180 degrees while descending in the same plane used during the climb.

Emergency Maneuvers and Introduction to Aerobatic Flight
The Spin

A SPIN DIFFERS FROM other aerobatic maneuvers because it is initiated by a stall. Increasing the angle of attack until lift is lost and lowering a wing. The difference in lift and drag between the lowered and raised wing turns the plane into a propeller, producing a feedback loop. The spin is possibly one of the most dangerous flight situations as the pilot can become disoriented. With the plane in a stall, the control surfaces have little or no effect. The situation fools the pilot's brain so recovery can only be achieved through training, doing what was learned instead of what logic dictates. In most dangerous situations power is applied and altitude gained, but doing this in a spin will worsen things, accelerating the uncontrolled descent. If the control stick is used to try to level out, the rotation will instantly change direction without stopping the fall.

To recover from a spin, the first thing to do is remain calm, reduce throttle and center all controls - this is often enough for the aircraft to complete one more turn before resuming normal flight. Most flight manuals propose applying opposite rudder until rotation stops.

Emergency Maneuvers and Introduction to Aerobatic Flight
Barrel Roll

THIS MANEUVER INVOLVES a 360 degree roll around the vertical axis while keeping the aircraft's nose on the same horizontal path. It is important to slightly raise the nose before initiating the maneuver. Depending on the aircraft model, speed, and the force applied to the controls by the pilot, barrel rolls of varying sizes can be executed, even lining up on top of the longitudinal axis. The barrel roll was used in both evasion and attack, as it can be performed while keeping guns aimed at the enemy.

Emergency Maneuvers and Introduction to Aerobatic Flight
Loop

MOST AEROBATIC MANEUVERS are initiated with a barrel roll or spin. The loop is perhaps one of the best known. It involves a complete 360 degree circle along the transverse axis - pitching up to invert the aircraft and continuing the curve down until closing the circle. Far from what it may seem, completing a perfect circle has its challenges. Although performed by solely pulling back on the stick, some finesse is needed to round out the figure with adjustments to the stick and throttle. Holding the controls steady would at best result in an oval shape. Adding a barrel roll to this maneuver allowed the pursued aircraft to turn the tables in aerial combat, getting behind its enemy's tail.

Emergency Maneuvers and Introduction to Aerobatic Flight
Immelmann Turn

This maneuver begins with a loop and finishes with a half roll, changing direction - if the aircraft was heading north, upon completion it heads south while maintaining altitude. It combines five-eighths of a loop and half a roll. It served as an evasive tactic, causing pursuers to overshoot and suddenly find themselves ahead in the gunsights.

Emergency Maneuvers and Introduction to Aerobatic Flight
Half Cuban Eight

THE HALF CUBAN EIGHT combines half a loop and half a roll, changing both direction and altitude - for example, flying north at 400 meters could be turned into heading south at 500 meters. Mixing variants of these basic maneuvers served for both attacking and evading enemies. Remaining hidden by the sun's glare, performing a half Cuban eight to swiftly get behind the enemy's tail before opening fire.

DISTINTOS PARTICULARES Y EMPRESAS
(*) El oro se beneficiaba en las fundiciones murcianas, como producto secundario.
(**) Metal Bullón ó (***) Metal Dore

Año	Toneladas movidas	Kg. Oro obtenidos	Valor producción vendible (ptas.)
1.911	500	(*)	5.000
1.912	1.380	(*)	23.460
1.913	Sin datos	(*)	Sin datos
1.914	Sin datos	(*)	Sin datos
1.915	Sin datos	(*)	Sin datos
1.916	376	(*)	(Sin valorar)
1.917	50	(*)	650
1.918	Sin datos	(*)	Sin datos
1.919	Sin datos	(*)	Sin datos
1.920	10	(*)	765
1.921	292	(*)	5.256
1.922	1.937	(*)	96.650
1.923	620	(*)	31.000
1.924	260	(*)	13.000
1.925	1.745	(*)	(Sin valorar)
1.926	495	(*)	(Sin valorar)
TOTALES	**7.665**	**0**	**175.781**

MINAS DE RODALQUILAR S.A.

Año	Toneladas movidas	Kg. Oro obtenidos	Valor producción vendible (ptas.)
1.931	4.178	65	(Sin valorar)
1.932	11.250	128	562.500
1.933	18.241	240	1.920.000
1.934	20.838	236	1.890.928
1.935	20.479	242	1.938.928
1.936	15.517	133	1.203.730
TOTALES	**90.503**	**1044**	**7.516.086**

GUERRA CIVIL

Año	Toneladas movidas	Kg. Oro obtenidos	Valor producción vendible (ptas.)
1.937	6.004	41	332.144
1.938	265	29	234.520
1.939	110	0	0
TOTALES	**6.379**	**70**	**566.664**

INSTITUTO GEOLÓGICO Y MINERO DE ESPAÑA

Año	Toneladas movidas	Kg. Bullón obtenidos	Valor producción vendible (ptas.)
1.940	3.647	(**) 367	440.400
1.941	0	0	0
1.942	0	0	0
TOTALES	**3.647**	**367**	**440.400**

EMPRESA NACIONAL ADARO

Año	Toneladas movidas	Kg. Oro obtenidos	Valor producción vendible (ptas.)
1.943	2.740	0	0
1.944	7.500	28	392.000
1.945	24.000	Sin datos	1.254.400
1.946	20.700	104	2.080.000
1.947	21.230	84	2.110.750
1.948	20.382	155	3.875.000
1.949	7.855	624	23.377.055
1.950	12.780	60	3.626.520
1.951	21.414	102	5.641.075
1.952	22.988	65	3.588.750
1.953	22.905	66	5.660.000
1.954	21.675	88	4.860.240
1.955	25.513	104	5.714.995
1.956	63.074	159	9.542.340
1.957	177.381	367	22.020.000
1.958	202.860	442	23.145.750
1.959	172.939	474	32.667.407
1.960	154.365	435	28.272.962
1.961	135.978	256	18.147.302
1.962	66.653	208	14.638.508
1.963	76.127	486	33.228.980
1.964	69.299	732	49.889.402
1.965	59.399	258	17.558.956
1.966	4.824	13	1.259.000
1.967	0	0	0
TOTALES	**1.414.581**	**5.310**	**312.551.392**

ST. JOE TRANSACCION INC. Y CIA. S.R.C.

Año	Toneladas movidas	Kg. Oro obtenidos	Valor producción vendible (ptas.)
1.989	Sin datos	85	110.588.000
1.990	Sin datos	137	175.511.000
TOTALES	**Sin datos**	**222**	**286.099.000**

(***) 1989   85 Kg. Au + 16 kg. Ag
(***) 1990 137 Kg. Au + 25 kg. Ag
         222 Kg. Au   41 kg. Ag

Fuente: Hernández Ortiz, F. (2002). Sintetizado a partir de la Estadística Minera y Metalúrgica de España, años 1861-1996.

The price of 1 ounce of gold in 2023 is 1,890.36 US Dollars.

Did you love *Shooting Stars in the Summer Sky*? Then you should read *Commander Valentina Smirnova*[1] by Francisco Angulo de Lafuente!

[2]

Commander Valentina Smirnova

In an era when women had no voice or vote and were frowned upon outside of the kitchen, Valentina Smirnova flew her Polikarpov I-16 fighter plane fighting against Franco's Fascists, Mussolini's Fascists and Hitler's Nazis in the skies of war-torn Spain.

Russian snipers. The Nazis were losing their minds over those women.

Lyuba Vinogradova

At the end of this book an explanatory annex has been added, about basic combat flight maneuvers used at that time. The era of propellers, when piston engine aircraft - Hispano-Suiza, Daimler-Benz

1. https://books2read.com/u/3yQ7El

2. https://books2read.com/u/3yQ7El

or Rolls-Royce Merlin - dominated the skies. Although this is a historical novel documented on real events, both the plot and characters are fictitious. Some authentic details have been altered according to the needs of the fiction.

Read more at https://twitter.com/Francisco_Ecofa.

Also by Francisco Angulo de Lafuente

Destination Havana
Eco-fuel-FA (ECOFA) A viable solution
El Olfateador нюхальщик
Los Mejores (The Best)
То,что Вы не должны делать ,чтобы стать писателем

Compañía N°12
Destino La Habana - Destination Havana
EL OLFATEADOR
La leyenda de los Tarazashi
LÁZARO RIP
Estrella fugaces en el cielo de verano
Commander Valentina Smirnova
Escapando del Infierno
Comandante Valentina Smirnova
Freak - El Circo de los Horrores
INVADERS La invasión ha comenzado
The Sniffer
Una boda gitana y un funeral escocés
Freak - The Circus of Horrors
Escaping from Hell
Shooting Stars in the Summer Sky

Watch for more at https://twitter.com/Francisco_Ecofa.

Nagore M.

About the Author

Francisco Angulo Madrid, 1976

Enthusiast of fantasy cinema and literature and a lifelong fan of Isaac Asimov and Stephen King, Angulo starts his literary career by submitting short stories to different contests. At 17 he finishes his first book - a collection of poems – and tries to publish it. Far from feeling intimidated by the discouraging responses from publishers, he decides to push ahead and tries even harder.

In 2006 he published his first novel "The Relic", a science fiction tale that was received with very positive reviews. In 2008 he presented "Ecofa" an essay on biofuels, whereAngulorecounts his experiences in the research project he works on. In 2009 he published "Kira and the Ice Storm".A difficultbut very productive year, in2010 he completed "Eco-fuel-FA",a science book in English. He also worked on several literary projects: "The Best of 2009-2010", "The Legend of Tarazashi 2009-2010", "The Sniffer 2010", "Destination Havana 2010-2011" and "Company No.12".

He currently works as director of research at the Ecofa project. Angulo is the developer of the first 2nd generation biofuel obtained from organic waste fed bacteria. He specialises in environmental issues and science-fiction novels.

His expertise in the scientific field is reflected in the innovations and technological advances he talks about in his books, almost prophesying what lies ahead, as Jules Verne didin his time.

Francisco Angulo Madrid-1976

Gran aficionado al cine y a la literatura fantástica, seguidor de Asimov y de Stephen King, Comienza su andadura literaria presentando relatos cortos a diferentes certámenes. A los 17 años termina su primer libro, un poemario que intenta publicar sin éxito. Lejos de amedrentarse ante las respuestas desalentadoras de las editoriales, decide seguir adelante, trabajando con más ahínco.

Read more at https://twitter.com/Francisco_Ecofa.

Milton Keynes UK
Ingram Content Group UK Ltd.
UKHW040640040923
428018UK00001B/100